TRICKY TWENTY-TWO

Stephanie Plum might not be the world's greatest bounty hunter, but she knows when she's being played. Unofficial student leader Ken Globovic (aka Gobbles) has been arrested for beating up the dean of students at Kiltman College. Gobbles has missed his court date and gone into hiding. People have seen him on campus, but no one will talk. Stephanie can't shake the feeling that something funny is going on. As much as everyone loves Gobbles, they hate Doug Linken. When Linken is gunned down, the list of suspects is long. The only people who care about finding the killer are Trenton cop Joe Morelli, security expert Ranger — and Stephanie, who has her eye on a cash prize and hopefully some tricks up her sleeve . . .

SPECIAL MESSAGE TO READERS

THE ULVERSCROFT FOUNDATION
(registered UK charity number 264873)
was established in 1972 to provide funds for
research, diagnosis and treatment of eye diseases.
Examples of major projects funded by
the Ulverscroft Foundation are:-

- The Children's Eye Unit at Moorfields Eye Hospital, London
- The Ulverscroft Children's Eye Unit at Great Ormond Street Hospital for Sick Children
- Funding research into eye diseases and treatment at the Department of Ophthalmology, University of Leicester
- The Ulverscroft Vision Research Group, Institute of Child Health
- Twin operating theatres at the Western Ophthalmic Hospital, London
- The Chair of Ophthalmology at the Royal Australian College of Ophthalmologists

You can help further the work of the Foundation
by making a donation or leaving a legacy.
Every contribution is gratefully received. If you
would like to help support the Foundation or
require further information, please contact:

THE ULVERSCROFT FOUNDATION
The Green, Bradgate Road, Anstey
Leicester LE7 7FU, England
Tel: (0116) 236 4325

website: www.ulverscroft-foundation.org.uk

TRICKY TWENTY-TWO

JANET EVANOVICH

LARGE
PRINT

First published in Great Britain 2015
by Headline Review
an imprint of Headline Publishing Group

First Isis Edition
published 2020
by arrangement with
Headline Publishing Group
An Hachette UK Company

ISBN 978-1-78541-834-1 (hb)
ISBN 978-1-78541-840-2 (pb)

Published by
Ulverscroft Limited
Anstey, Leicestershire

Set by Words & Graphics Ltd.
Anstey, Leicestershire
Printed and bound in Great Britain by
T. J. International Ltd., Padstow, Cornwall

This book is printed on acid-free paper

CHAPTER
ONE

Ginny Scoot was standing on a third-floor ledge, threatening to jump, and it was more or less my fault. My name is Stephanie Plum and I work as a bounty hunter for my bail bondsman cousin Vinnie.

Ginny had failed to show for a court appearance and it was my job to find her and return her to the authorities. If I don't succeed my cousin is out his bond money, and I don't get paid. On the other hand, there's Ginny, who would prefer not to go back to jail.

My colleague Lula and I were on the sidewalk, looking up at Ginny, along with a bunch of other people who were taking video with their smartphones.

"This here's not a good angle for her," Lula said to me. "Everybody could look up her skirt and see her hoo-ha. I guess technically you could see her thong, but we all know her lady parts are lurkin' in there behind that little piece of red material and ass floss."

Lula was originally a respectable 'ho. A couple years ago she'd decided to relinquish her corner and take a job as file clerk for the bonds office. Since almost all the files are digital these days, Lula mostly works as my wheelman. She's four inches too short for her weight, her clothes are three sizes too small for her generously proportioned body, her hair color changes weekly, her skin is a robust dark chocolate.

I feel invisible when I stand next to Lula because no one notices me. I inherited a lot of unruly curly brown hair from the Italian side of my family, and I have a cute nose that my grandma says is a gift from God. My blue eyes and pale skin are the results of my mother's Hungarian heritage. Not sure where my 34B boobs came from, but I'm happy with them, and I think they look okay with the rest of me.

Just ten minutes ago I'd almost had the cuffs on Ginny. Lula and I were at her door, and I was giving her the usual bounty hunter baloney.

"We need to take you downtown so you can reschedule your court date," I'd said to Ginny. "It won't take long."

This was partly true. The rescheduling went quickly. Whether she would make bail again was a whole other issue. If she didn't make bail she'd be a guest of the penal system until she came up to trial.

"Screw you," Ginny said, and she flicked her Big Gulp at me, slammed her door shut, and locked it.

By the time Lula and I got the door unlocked Ginny had climbed out her bedroom window and was standing on a two-foot-wide ledge. So here I was, in a soaking wet shirt, trying to talk Ginny off the ledge.

"Okay," I yelled at her. "I'm out of your apartment. That's what you wanted, right? Go back inside."

"I don't want to go to jail."

2

"It's not that bad," Lula told her. "They let you watch television in the dayroom, and you'll make new friends."

"I'd rather die," Ginny said. "I'm going to jump."

"Yeah, but you're only on the third floor," Lula said. "You'll just break a bunch of bones. And anyways you never know about these court cases. Sometimes they get dismissed."

"She cut off her boyfriend's penis," I whispered to Lula.

"It could have been justified," Lula said.

"It was his *penis*!"

"So probably chances of him dismissing the charges aren't so good," Lula said. "Men don't like when you cut their dick off. I hear it's real hard to sew a dick back on.

"If you want to die you have to make sure you land on your head," Lula yelled up to Ginny. "That probably would do it."

Two Trenton PD squad cars drove up and parked at an angle to the curb. They were followed by a fire truck and an EMS truck.

One of the uniforms from the squad car came over to talk to me.

"What's going on?"

"She's FTA," I told him. "I went to cuff her, and she managed to get away and get out on the ledge."

A satellite truck from the local television station pulled up behind the fire truck.

"Can you get someone to talk to her? A relative or her boyfriend?" the cop asked me.

3

"Probably not the boyfriend," I said.

The fire department put a bounce bag on the sidewalk under the window, and a cameraman from the SAT truck started to set up.

"You're not gonna look photogenic when you hit that bounce bag, what with your short skirt and all," Lula yelled at Ginny. "You might want to rethink this."

Joe Morelli sidled up to me. He's a homicide detective with the Trenton PD. He's six foot tall with a lot of lean, hard muscle, wavy black hair, and a smile that makes a girl want to take her clothes off. I've known Morelli all my life, and lately he's been my boyfriend.

"Looks like you've got a jumper," Morelli said.

"Vinnie bonded her out, and she went FTA," I told him. "I was about to cuff her, and she ran for the ledge."

"What's her charge?"

"She cut off her boyfriend's pecker," Lula said.

This got a grimace out of Morelli and the uniform.

"Maybe you can talk to her," I said to Morelli.

Morelli had gone from a bad kid to a petty officer in the Navy, and had become a really great cop. He's smart. He's compassionate. He believes in the law, the American dream, and the inherent goodness of human beings. If you break the law or step on the American dream, he'll root you out like a wolverine going after a ground squirrel. He has a house, a dog, a toaster, and a level of maturity I suspect I haven't yet obtained. The men in his family are drunks and womanizers and abusive. Morelli is none of those. He's movie star

4

handsome in a Jersey Italian kind of way, and he oozes testosterone. And from the first time he was able to put a sentence together he's had a reputation for being able to talk a woman into doing anything. He got to peek at my cotton Tinker Bell underpants when I was a little kid, and he relieved me of the burden of my virginity when I was in high school. It seemed to me that sending Morelli up to the third floor to talk a woman off a ledge was a no-brainer.

"Is she armed?" Morelli asked me.

"I don't think so."

"No butcher knives? Paring knives? Box cutters?"

"Didn't see any."

He disappeared into the building, and a couple minutes later I saw him at the window. Ginny inched away from him, beyond his grasp. The fire guys moved the bounce bag over to accommodate her. I couldn't hear what he was saying, but I saw her smile. They talked a little longer, she nodded agreement, and inched back toward him. He reached out for her, and when she tried to take his hand she lost her balance, slipped off the ledge, and plummeted to the ground. She hit the bounce bag with a solid *thud* and didn't move. The EMTs immediately converged on her.

Everyone watching took a sharp intake of air and went silent, focused on the EMTs. I felt Morelli move in behind me, his hand on my shoulder. And suddenly Ginny sat up.

"I'm okay!" Ginny said. "Wow, that was a rush. I bet I could be a stunt girl in the movies."

Morelli motioned an EMT over to us.

5

"Is she going to be okay?" Morelli asked.

"She just had the air knocked out of her. We'll transport her to St. Francis Hospital to get checked out and then she'll be released."

"She's going to need a police escort," Morelli said to the uniform who was still with us. "When she's done at St. Francis she gets booked downtown."

"Boy, for a minute there that was a heart stopper," Lula said. "I don't even want to hear anything go *thud* like that again. That made my stomach feel sick. I need a burger and fries. And then I'm going home on account of my favorite television shows are coming on." Lula looked over at Morelli and looked back at me. "Do you need me to take you home or are you going with Officer Hottie?"

"I'll take her home," Morelli said.

Lula left, and I followed Morelli to his car. "How did you happen to turn up here?"

"Dumb luck. I had dinner with Anthony, and I was on my way home when I saw Lula's Firebird parked half a block from a disaster scene. I thought chances were good you'd be involved."

Anthony is Morelli's brother. He's married to a woman who keeps divorcing him and then remarrying him. Every time they get remarried she gets pregnant. I've lost count of how many kids Anthony has, but his house is bedlam.

"Thanks for helping out," I said to Morelli.

"I wasn't much help. I almost got your FTA killed."

Morelli opened the door to his SUV and his dog, Bob, bounded out and almost knocked me over. Bob is

6

a huge shaggy-haired orange dog that mostly resembles a golden retriever. I got a lot of dog kisses, Bob and I wrestled over who was going to sit in the front seat next to Morelli, and I won.

"Your house or mine?" Morelli asked.

"Yours. My television isn't working. You have to drop me at the office first so I can get my car."

Morelli had inherited a nice little house from his Aunt Rose. It's just over the line from my parents' house in the Burg, and if you didn't know the line existed you would think Morelli lived in the Burg. Houses are modest but neatly maintained. Cars are washed every Saturday. Flags are displayed on appropriate holidays. Veterans and cops are revered. Even if you belong to the mob you still appreciate and respect veterans and cops. Hardworking people live in these neighborhoods, and they look to the police to protect their hard-earned civil liberties and flat-screens. If prejudice exists it is kept behind closed doors. Out in public everyone qualifies equally for getting the finger.

When Morelli first moved into the house it was all Aunt Rose. Now, with the exception of the upstairs bedroom curtains, the house is Morelli. Small living room, dining room, kitchen, and powder room downstairs. Three small bedrooms and one full bath upstairs. He has a single-car garage that he never uses. And he has a backyard where Bob practices digging and pooping.

It was almost nine when Morelli, Bob, and I rolled into the house and made our way to the kitchen.

Morelli pulled leftover pizza out of the fridge and divided it up among the three of us. Bob ate his on the spot, and Morelli and I took ours into the living room to eat in front of the TV. It was early September, and Morelli went with a Mets game. We finished the pizza, and before the Mets could get through an inning Morelli had his hand on my leg and his tongue in my mouth. This wasn't a shocking surprise. We'd been casually cohabitating with the occasional mention of love and marriage. He kept condoms at my house, and I kept tampons at his house, but that was as much as we'd moved in so far.

We migrated to the bedroom and didn't bother with a lot of the preliminaries since we'd already done that downstairs while the Mets were changing pitchers.

Morelli is an unpredictable lover. Sometimes he's slow and thoughtful. Sometimes he's almost violent with need. Sometimes he's funny. Frequently he's all three. Once in a while when we try to make love while the Giants are playing the Patriots he's a little distracted. I felt like this was one of those distracted nights, but without the Giants.

We were cuddled together in postcoital lethargy, and I wondered about Morelli's thoughts. What was the source of the distraction? Murder, mayhem, marriage? Suppose it was marriage. What would I say? Things had been really good between us lately. I might say yes! Then again, I might not be ready. Marriage was a huge commitment. And there would be children. I suppose I could manage children. I'm pretty good at taking care of my hamster, Rex. I gave up a sigh. Probably I would have to accept his proposal. He would be crushed if I didn't. His police work might suffer. He'd be depressed and demoralized. He'd have self-doubt.

"About tonight," I said to him. "You seem a little distracted."

"I have a lot on my mind."

I tried not to smile too much. I was pretty sure this was it. I wondered if he had a ring.

"Would you like to talk about it?" I asked him.

"There's not much I can say right now, but I think we should cool this off for a while and date other people."

"Yes. *What?*"

"I'm thinking about a lifestyle change, and I need to be uninvolved while I figure it out," Morelli said. "So I'm giving you the freedom to look around. As long as you don't look around with Ranger."

Carlos Manoso, mostly known as Ranger, owns Rangeman, an elite security firm located in a stealth building downtown. He's former Special Forces, former badass bounty hunter, and he was my mentor when I started working for Vinnie. He's dark. He's smart. He plays by his own rules, and I don't have a complete copy of his rule book. Morelli thinks Ranger is a loose cannon and bad influence, and Morelli is right.

"*Seriously?*" I said, sitting up, rigid, eyes bulging out of their sockets.

"I've been thinking about it for a while."

"And this is the time you pick to spring it on me?"

"Is this a bad time?"

I was on my feet. Arms waving in the air. Outrage steaming off the top of my head. "I'm naked. You don't give a woman this sort of information when she's naked. What the heck are you thinking?"

"It might be temporary."

"*Might* be *temporary?* As in but it's *probably permanent?* Adios. Goodbye. Are you freaking kidding me?" I narrowed my eyes at him. "Do you have someone special in mind that you want to date?"

"No."

"Omigod, you're going to the other side. You're gay."

"Not even a little."

"My friend Bobby says the only difference between a gay man and a straight man is a six-pack of beer."

"Cupcake, after six beers I'm not worth much of anything to anybody."

"So what kind of life change are you thinking about?"

"I'm thinking about a career change. Not being a cop."

"Wow."

"Yeah. Shocker, right?"

I kicked through the clothes on the floor, looking for my underwear. "What will you do?"

"Don't know." He crooked a finger at me. "Come back to bed."

"You just dumped me and now you think I'm going to hop back into bed with you? Are you insane?"

"We can still be friends."

"I'm not feeling friendly. I'm feeling angry." I zipped up my jeans and grabbed my T-shirt off the floor. "And

I certainly don't sleep with men after they dump me. Okay, maybe once in a while, but not usually. And I'm absolutely not sleeping with you. Not *ever again*." I hooked my tote bag over my shoulder and huffed out of Morelli's bedroom.

"I'll call you in the morning," Morelli yelled after me.

I gave him the finger as I stomped down the stairs. He couldn't see me, but it was satisfying all the same. I slammed the front door shut with enough force to rattle his living room windows, marched over to my crap-ass car, and rammed myself behind the wheel. I peeled away from the curb and drove to the all-night convenience store on Hamilton Avenue. I bought a load of comfort food and went home to eat it. Snickers bars, Reese's Peanut Butter Cups, York Peppermint Patties, M&M's, Twizzlers, everything I could find that contained caramel, plus three tubs of ice cream.

CHAPTER
TWO

My cousin Vinnie owns the bail bonds office, but his wife's father, Harry the Hammer, owns Vinnie. Vinnie writes most of the bonds, plays the ponies, likes to get whipped once in a while by dark-skinned young men, and in general is a boil on the backside of my family tree.

Connie Rosolli occupies the guard dog desk outside Vinnie's private office. She keeps the office running, occasionally writes bonds, and makes sure no one kills Vinnie during office hours. She's in her midthirties, is longtime divorced, and looks like a short, Italian, bigger-boobed Cher.

"Whoa," Connie said when I dragged myself into the office Monday morning. "You look like you got hit by a train. You have black circles under your eyes and a big pimple on your chin."

"I broke up with Morelli last night." I put my finger to the pimple. It felt like Mount Rainier. "I think this is a candy pimple. I went through a lot of Snickers last night. And then I had a bag of Oreos for breakfast."

Lula was on the couch. "Oreos don't work for breakfast," Lula said. "You need something like a

Almond Joy so you get the protein in the nut. You eat Oreos and you just get Oreo poop."

Lula was wearing ankle boots with studs and five-inch spike heels, a black spandex skirt that barely covered her butt, a poison green tank top that was stretched to its limit over her big boobs, and a sparkly, fluffy, pink angora cardigan. Every time she moved, some of the angora floated off the sweater and swirled in the air.

"So what's the deal with Morelli?" Lula asked. "He's a hottie. You sure you want to break up with him?"

"He broke up with me. And I don't want to talk about it."

"It was before the pimple though, right?" Lula asked.

"Yeah."

"Well, then, we can rule that out."

The door to Vinnie's inner office banged open and Vinnie stuck his head out.

"What's going on out here?" Vinnie said. "I'm not paying you to stand around flapping your lips." He leaned forward and squinted at me. "What the hell is that thing on your chin?"

"It's a pimple," Lula said. "She got some stress in her life."

"Cripes," Vinnie said. "It's a freakin' nightmare. It looks like Vesuvius is gonna erupt." And he pulled back into his office, closed and locked his door.

"I had a new FTA come in late yesterday afternoon," Connie said. "A kid who didn't show for his court date. I made some phone calls, and he's definitely in the wind." She handed the file over to me. "Ken Globovic,

13

aka Gobbles. Twenty-one years old. College guy. Breaking and entering and aggravated assault."

Lula looked over my shoulder as I paged through the file.

"It says here this moron attacked the dean of students," Lula said. "I imagine this cut his college career short. I'm no college graduate, but I know you're not supposed to try to kill the dean of students."

I looked at his picture. Sandy blond hair, fair skin, a little pudgy. Kind of cute in an albino chipmunk sort of way.

"He don't look like no killer," Lula said. "He looks like he wears Winnie-the-Pooh jammies to bed at night."

"He's a Zeta," Connie said. "So you might want to start at the Zeta house."

"*Zeta house*. That sounds like a nice place," Lula said.

"It's either the best or the worst fraternity on campus, depending on your point of view. The Zeta house is better known as *the zoo*," Connie said. "Draw your own conclusions. And Ken Globovic holds the title of *the Supreme Exalted Zookeeper*. Last month the Zetas dumped a load of Alka-Seltzer into a rival fraternity's water system and all their toilets exploded. They said it was a chemistry experiment and inspired by the movie *Animal House*."

"I bet they got a A on that one," Lula said. "I would have given them a A."

I shoved the file into my messenger bag. "Anything else come in?"

14

"No, but Billy Brown is still out there, and he's a medium bond. It would be good to get that money back."

Billy Brown, now known far and wide as Billy Bacon, made national news when he greased himself up with bacon fat and broke into a multimillion-dollar home by sliding down the chimney. He set the alarm off on his way out and was attacked by a bacon-loving pack of dogs before he was able to get to his car. When the police rescued him they found $10,000 in jewelry and $5,000 in cash stuffed into his various pockets. Vinnie was dumb enough to bond him out, and no one's seen Billy Bacon since.

"I'll keep my eyes open," I said. "I'll do another drive through his neighborhood."

"I'll go with you," Lula said. "As I remember he lived on K Street, and they got a deli that makes excellent egg salad. They put chopped-up olives in it and use lots of mayonnaise. Mayonnaise is the secret to a good egg salad. And you never can go wrong with olives. We could time our investigation so that it coincides with lunch. And before we go anywhere you might want to put some concealer on that pimple, so people don't go screaming in horror and run away when they see you up close."

We took Lula's car because she drives a red Firebird that's in pristine condition while my car, which I'm pretty sure used to be a Ford Something, is a rust bucket.

15

"We're going to Kiltman College, right?" Lula asked. "You know what they call it? They call it *Clitman*. I mean, who'd wanna go to a school they call *Clitman*? If I had my choice I'd go to Rider. That's a better name for a school. I mean I'm all in favor of acknowledgin' ladies' special parts, but I don't want it on my diploma, if you see what I'm saying."

I was in favor of acknowledging special parts too, but I didn't want to talk about them. I was raised Catholic, and talking about *special parts* with Lula made my stomach feel a little icky. Truth is, I had a hard time with the blind-faith part of Catholicism, but I was very good at holding on to Catholic guilt.

"I'd rather not talk about the you-know-what," I said to Lula.

"Boy, there's lots you don't want to talk about today. You don't want to talk about why you got dumped neither. I'm guessing it was a surprise. When did this happen? Last night? Maybe it's on account of you're sexually repressed."

"I'm not sexually repressed."

"You don't want to talk about any of your special parts even though they've been brought into the mainstream lately. Ladies' special parts are big news now."

"That doesn't mean I'm sexually repressed."

"It don't mean nothing good, neither. So when did he dump you? Did he dump you after you did the deed? 'Cause that's never a good sign. That could mean there was something lacking in your performance."

16

I was thinking it was a good thing I'd left my gun at home in my cookie jar because if I had it with me I might shoot Lula.

"On the other hand, he could have asked for something unreasonable," Lula said. "If that's the case then good riddance is what I say. Like I don't do none of that butt stuff no more."

"Good God."

"Exactly. It's against human nature. I have my standards. And, okay, so some playful spanking is allowed, but, honey, you better not leave a welt. You leave a welt on my booty, and you'll have Firebird tire treads on your ass."

"I don't want to know any of this," I said to Lula.

"Well, I'm just sayin'. I keep my skin silky soft with lanolin, and I don't want no welts. What's the world coming to when a girl allows for welts on her booty?"

Kiltman College sits on the northwestern edge of Trenton. It's a medium-sized school known for academic excellence in the sciences, turning a blind eye toward fraternity debauchery, and for having the youngest *Jeopardy!* champion, wunderkind and biology prodigy Avi Attar, enrolled in its undergraduate honors program.

Lula drove through the campus and parked in front of the Zeta house. It was a large two-story building with peeling white paint and a ragged couch on the patchy front lawn. There was a sign over the door that originally said "Zeta" but the Z had mostly flaked off so it now read "eta". The door had been propped open with a folding chair, and the smell of stale beer rushed out the open door.

"These Zeta people need a air freshener," Lula said.

Two guys were slouched on a couch in a common area, watching SpongeBob on a big flat-screen television. I introduced myself and told them I was looking for Ken Globovic.

"Don't know him," the one guy said.

"He belongs to this fraternity," I told him.

"Hunh," the guy said. "Imagine that." He elbowed the guy next to him. "Hey, Iggy, do you know someone named Ken Globovic?"

"Nuh-unh," Iggy said.

"Cute," Lula said. "How about I sit on you and see if that helps your memory?"

"Haw," Iggy said. "You gonna lap dance me, momma?"

"No," Lula said. "I'm gonna squash you like a bug. And before I squash you, I'm gonna let Stephanie here punch you in the face."

I tried to look threatening, but honestly I wasn't real big on punching people in the face. I bitch-slapped Joyce Barnhardt once. And I'd kicked a man in the knee last week, but he was armed, and he deserved to get kicked.

Iggy looked up at me. "What's that thing on your face? Is that a pimple?"

"I've been under some stress lately," I said.

"I can identify," Iggy said. "You want a beer?"

"No, thank you," I said.

Four more guys wandered over.

18

"These ladies are looking for someone named Ken Globovic," Iggy said. "Any of you know him?"

"Who?"

"Not me."

"Nope."

"So you won't mind if I poke around the house," I said.

"Poke all you want," Iggy said. "The Zetas have nothing to hide."

"Yeah," one of them said. "We're happy to show you everything we got. You want to see what we got now?"

Lula leaned in. "You want to see what *I* got?"

They all thought about it for a beat, and shook their heads no.

"Globovic listed the Zeta house as his address," I said. "Someone want to show me his room?"

They shuffled around and shrugged their shoulders.

"Guess we gotta go room by room then," Lula said. "Just to make it official we might bring Stephanie's ex-boyfriend with us. He's a cop and you might have to worry about him finding some illegal weed and stuff."

"Not necessary," Iggy said, coming off the couch. "Follow me."

Iggy led the way, Lula and I followed, and the remaining five guys followed Lula and me. We walked out of the room, up a wide winding staircase, and down a long hallway. There was a guy standing at attention in front of an open door. He was wearing a dress.

"Sirs," he said as we passed.

"He's a pledge," Iggy said to Lula and me.

"Why's he wearing a dress?" Lula asked.

"It part of our gender sensitivity training," Iggy said.

"Yeah, but I might be offended by that because the color is all wrong for him and that dress got some wrinkles in it," Lula said.

"Someone get a paddle and give that pledge a whack for having wrinkles in his dress," Iggy said.

A guy peeled off the pack, and a moment later we heard *whack!*

"*Ow!*"

"He's gonna have a welt," Lula said. "He should have ironed his dress."

I cut my eyes to her. "He would have been fine if you hadn't said something."

"Well, I just noticed, is all. You think I should tell him about lanolin?"

"No!"

Iggy stopped in front of a room and motioned us in. "Nobody home here," Iggy said.

I methodically went through the room, looking in drawers, the closet, under the bed. Some of Globovic's books and clothes were strewn about the room, but the toiletries had been removed from the bathroom. There wasn't a smartphone lying out. No computer or tablet. It was clear Globovic wasn't staying here, but I didn't find a forwarding address.

"I don't suppose anyone wants to tell me where I can find Globovic, or Gobbles, if that's what you call him."

No one came forward.

CHAPTER
THREE

We left the Zeta house and got back into the Firebird.

"That was a big waste of time," Lula said. "And they were all fibbing about not knowing where Gobbles is hiding out. I figure he's in the cellar."

I had the same thought, but I didn't want to go into the Zeta house cellar. I was afraid it would be a dungeon where they kept the cross-dressing pledges. Or even worse, it could be filled with spiders.

"There's a story here," I said to Lula. "This guy has no priors. He's a good student. I didn't see anything weird in his room. His fraternity brothers obviously like him, because they're protecting him. His family hired a good lawyer for him, but he chose to disappear and not show up for court."

"Yeah, but that's typical of a amateur," Lula said. "Everybody's afraid to go to jail for the first time. Especially if they got freaked out over getting arrested and locked up overnight in one of them cells at the police station. And it's not like he got friends and relatives already in jail waiting for him like most of the people in my neighborhood. In my neighborhood the only way you can afford to get dental work done is to get yourself sent to the workhouse for a couple months.

So it's not like it's perceived as a bad thing, you see what I'm saying?"

I read through Globovic's file again. His parents lived about an hour away in East Brunswick. I'd get to them eventually, but I wanted to run through the local connections first.

"Globovic was accused of attacking the dean of students," I said to Lula, "so let's talk to him next."

After ten minutes of confused driving around the Kiltman campus, Lula managed to find the administration building.

"This school must have been built around cow paths," Lula said, pulling into the lot and finding an empty space to park. "There's no signs on any of the little roads, and GPS don't know nothing."

The campus was mostly composed of big blocky redbrick buildings. Two or three floors for all but the science building, which looked brand-new and was five stories. The administration building was fancied up by four columns marching across the front.

Martin Mintner, the dean of students, had an office on the second floor. A small waiting area in front of his office held four uncomfortable wooden chairs and a scarred wood coffee table with a couple dog-eared magazines on it.

"This must be where the bad kids get sent," Lula said.

The door to the dean's office was open, so I stuck my head in. "Knock, knock."

The man behind the desk was slightly paunchy with dark hair cut short. Receding hairline. Gray beginning to show at the temples. I guessed he was in his early fifties. He was wearing a light blue buttoned-down shirt with a gray and red repp tie. He had a cast on his left forearm.

He looked up from his computer at me. "Yes?"

"Dean Mintner?"

"Can I help you?"

"I hope so," I said. "I'm looking for Ken Globovic."

Red spots instantly appeared on Mintner's cheeks. "What exactly is this in reference to?"

"I work for Vincent Plum Bail Bonds," I said. "Mr Globovic has missed his court date, and I need to locate him."

"Bounty hunter?" Mintner asked.

"Bond enforcement."

Mintner nodded. "Of course. He should never have been released from jail. He's a maniac. Broke into my house and came after me with a baseball bat. Broke my arm and practically totaled my living room."

"Was the bat his only weapon?"

"So far as I know," Mintner said. "I imagine all the details are in the police report."

"Why did he come after you?"

"I don't know," Mintner said. "Because he's a maniac? He just burst through the door and rushed at me. I didn't get a chance to ask him why he was trying to kill me."

"He must have been unhappy about something," Lula said.

"He's a Zeta," Mintner said. "They're all troublemakers. It's the fraternity from hell. The school has been trying to close it for years, but the Zeta alums are big contributors to the endowment."

"We were just there," Lula said. "It seemed like a nice place, except for the guy in the dress getting whacked with the paddle."

Mintner looked like he wanted to pop a couple Xanax. "They're all perverts," he said. "A bunch of sickos. I'd have the house burned to the ground, but they'd only rebuild. And Globovic is the worst. He's the ringleader. He's the mastermind for all the depravation. Every sick toga party springs out of his sick brain."

"You'd never know from his picture," Lula said. "He looks like that Winnie-the-Pooh kid, Christopher Robin."

"I want him found and locked up for the rest of his life," Mintner said. "Or at least until he's too old and decrepit to find my house."

"Do you have any ideas where I should start looking?" I asked him.

"I'm sure he hasn't gone far. He has connections here. Friends. Misguided people who want to help him. And there's something going on at the Zeta house. Something evil. And Globovic is involved."

"Whoa," Lula said. "Evil? You mean like demons and the devil?"

Mintner looked over at me. "Who is she?"

"That's Lula," I said.

"I'm her assistant," Lula said. "We're like the Lone Ranger and What's-His-Name."

I gave Mintner my card and told him to call me if he heard anything about Globovic.

"So what did you think of him?" Lula asked when we were out of the building.

"He doesn't like the Zeta house."

"Do you think there's something evil going on there?"

"*Evil* is a pretty strong word. Sometimes people say evil when they mean bad."

"I don't like evil," Lula said. "Evil gives me the creepy crawlies. I saw a movie once where a woman was possessed by a evil spirit and the woman's head would spin around and she'd vomit up cockroaches. One day she was perfectly normal, and then *bam!* she's vomiting up cockroaches. All because of this evil spirit. And in the movie that evil spirit was lurking in a house that looked sort of like the Zeta house."

"You're making that up."

"Swear to God. It was like that in the movie. I might think twice about going back into the Zeta house. I'm telling you, vomiting up cockroaches isn't on my bucket list." Lula looked at her watch. "Where are we going next? You think it's too early to get some egg salad?"

We were standing in front of the administration building, looking across a large green lawn that was sprinkled with college kids walking to classes, catching Frisbees, or sprawled out napping in the sun. The new building that housed the biology department was on the other side of the lawn.

"Globovic was a biology major," I said to Lula. "Let's try the biology department. Connie's done some preliminary research for me, so I have the name of Globovic's advisor, Stanley Pooka."

My cellphone buzzed with a text message from Ranger.

Need date. Pick you up at seven. Wear sexy red dress. Bring loaded gun.

This wasn't wonderful. I didn't need Ranger complicating my life right now. And I had a gun but I wasn't sure if I had any bullets.

"Bad news?" Lula asked.

"Ranger needs a date, and he's picking me up at seven."

"Why don't I ever get news like that? That's my kind of news. That man is so hot I get a flash just thinking about him." Lula fanned herself. "I feel warm all over. I hope it's not because I got possessed back there in the evil house."

"Maybe you're warm because it's almost eighty degrees and we're standing in the sun."

"Yeah, that could be it, but if I start horkin' up cockroaches you gotta get me to a priest."

We walked across the grass to the science building and took the elevator to Stanley Pooka's third-floor office. The office door was open, and I could see a man pacing inside. He was medium height and slender, and his yellow mass of frizzed, bushed-out hair looked like it could have squirrels hiding in it. He was waving his arms and talking to himself. Hard to tell his age. Maybe in his early fifties. He was wearing what appeared to be pajama bottoms, a gray T-shirt, and a large amulet on a chain around his neck.

26

"I think there's some nutjob in Professor Pooka's office," Lula said.

I moved into the doorway. "Professor Pooka?"

He whirled around. "Yes," he said. "Office hours are Wednesdays and Thursdays. This is Monday. Go away."

I introduced myself, gave him my card, and told him I was looking for Ken Globovic.

"He isn't here," Pooka said. "Your card says bond enforcement. How do I know you're really bond enforcement? Where's your gun? Why aren't you dressed in black leather?"

"Honey, black leather is so yesterday's television," Lula said. "We don't go with that black leather stuff no more, but I got a gun. It's a big one, too." Lula pawed through her purse, looking for her gun. "I know it's in here somewhere."

"You're Ken's advisor," I said to Pooka.

"I *was* his advisor. He's disappeared. Good riddance. He was a screwup anyway. Everyone at this school is a screwup."

"He belonged to Zeta," I said.

Pooka narrowed his eyes. "And? Are you implying something?"

"Nope," I said. "Just looking for answers."

"Then you're in the wrong place. No one wants answers here. This school is the work of the devil."

"Heard that before," Lula said.

"Academic freedom is dead here," Pooka said.

"Looks to me like what they got is freedom to spank," Lula said, still pawing around in her purse. "I can't find my gun. I must have left it in my other purse.

27

I changed it at the last minute on account of it wasn't complementary with my pink sweater. I'm careful about my accessorizing."

"Pink is a feminist color," Pooka said to Lula. "Are you a feminist?"

"You bet your ass," Lula said. "Unless I need something done that's man's work. Like relocating a snake. Then I'm all about bending the rules. Just 'cause I wear pink don't mean I'm stupid. And while we're on the subject of fashion, I have to tell you the necklace you're wearing is excellent."

"It's my power amulet," Pooka said. "I never take it off. It's the only protection I have from the evils of this school. To take it off would be an insult to the amulet."

"Yeah, and you don't want to insult your power amulet," Lula said. "It probably could do all kinds of shit. It might make your dick fall off. I saw an episode of *South Park* once where this guy drank gluten and his dick flew off."

"Excuse me," I said to Pooka. "Getting back to Ken Globovic. Do you have any idea where I might find him?"

"Try talking to his girlfriend. She's one of those activist nuts. Writes stupid things for the school paper."

"Do you know her name?"

"Don't know her name, but she looks like Malibu Barbie."

"Do you know Barbie don't wear no underpants?" Lula said. "I bought one for my niece and that doll didn't have no underpants. I mean, what kind of message is that to someone? She had something sort of

28

drawn on her molded plastic butt that might have looked like underpants, but it's not the same, you see what I'm saying? And she didn't have no bra, either. 'Course she don't need one on account of she's got perky plastic titties."

"Anything other than the girlfriend?" I asked Pooka.

"Talk to Avi. He's usually in the lab down the hall. He knows everyone. All the undergrads go to him for help with their projects."

"He's the wonder kid, right?" Lula asked. "I hear he's a real cutie."

"Girls love him," Pooka said. "They line up outside the lab. I think it's his hair. He has good hair."

Lula and I walked down the hall to the lab.

"I don't see any girls here," Lula said. "Must be a slow day for the wonder kid."

I'd had basic biology in high school and two semesters of microbiology in college. I'd hated every second of every class. I hated the way the labs smelled. I hated growing ick in the petri dishes, test tubes, and glass beakers. And I'd set my lab coat on fire trying to light my Bunsen burner . . . twice.

A slim, nice-looking teen was perched on a stool, working at a laptop. He was wearing a T-shirt and jeans and running shoes. He was the only one in the lab.

"Avi?" I asked him.

"Yes."

"I represent Vincent Plum Bail Bonds, and I'm looking for Ken Globovic."

"Everyone calls him Gobbles," Avi said. "I haven't seen him since he was arrested."

"Do you have any idea where he might be hiding?"

"No, but I suspect he's in the area. There have been sightings of him on campus. Mostly late at night."

"I was told he has a girlfriend."

"Julie Ruley," Avi said. "She's really nice. I think she's a journalism major. She came here with Gobbles a couple times."

"So what do you think of this Gobbles guy?" Lula asked him.

"I like him. And I can't see him breaking into Dean Mintner's house without good cause, if that's what you want to know."

I gave him my card and told him to call or text if Gobbles turned up.

Three girls were loitering in the hall when we left the lab.

"I can see why the ladies like him," Lula said. "Besides being cute, he's got a nice way about him."

"Charismatic."

"Yeah, that's it. Charismatic. Gobbles sounds like he's charismatic too. And I could tell you who *isn't* charismatic. It's that Dean Mintner. He don't sound like no fun at all. And if you ask me, Professor Pooka is batshit crazy."

"I'd like to talk to the girlfriend," I said to Lula.

"How're you going to find her?"

"The dean of students is going to help us."

"Oh boy, that's gonna be a treat. You sure you don't want to go after Billy Bacon first? Get ourselves fortified with egg salad before talking to Mr Cranky Pants again?"

30

"No. I want to get this wrapped up. If we can get one decent lead, this guy shouldn't be hard to snag. He's an amateur, and I'm sure the police confiscated his baseball bat. How hard can this be?"

I looked in at Mintner and did a little finger wave. "Hi. Remember me?"

Mintner was behind his desk. He leaned forward and squinted at me. "Yes. Now what?"

"I was hoping you could help me find Mr Globovic's girlfriend, Julie Ruley."

"Unfortunately I know this young woman," Mintner said. "She's trying to turn the school paper into the *Enquirer*. Everything is a crusade. It's all so sensational. And she has tattoos."

"Well, that's a sin against nature right there," Lula said.

"Exactly," Mintner said. He focused on Lula. "Are you being sarcastic? Do you have tattoos?"

"I don't have any tattoos on account of they don't show up that good on my fabulous dark chocolate skin. And yeah, I'm being sarcastic as hell."

Mintner mumbled something that I thought might have sounded like *dumb bitch* and turned to his computer. He typed in *Julie Ruley*, and moments later printed out her class schedule and dorm address.

"After classes she's most likely at the newspaper office," Mintner said. "I'm helping you because Globovic is a menace. He needs to be found and taken off the streets."

"You bet your ass," Lula said. "And we're the ladies who are gonna do it."

I took the printout and thanked Mintner. I picked up a campus map on the way out of the building and studied it. The newspaper office wasn't listed, but I guessed it would be either in the journalism department or in the student center. According to Julie Ruley's schedule she was currently in a twentieth-century literature class in the Steinart building. No doubt doing an in-depth comparison of James Joyce's *Ulysses* with *Harry Potter*.

"She's in class now," I said to Lula. "Then she's free for the afternoon. Since we don't know what she looks like, beyond being Malibu Barbie with tattoos, I guess we should try the newspaper office after lunch."

CHAPTER
FOUR

K Street is in a sketchy part of town. Not nearly as bad as the blighted blocks of upper Stark, but bad enough that you want to keep your eyes open for big mutant rats and drugged-out old men. Mixed in with the rats and the dopers are decent citizens, illegal immigrants, human traffickers, and runaway kids. Billy Bacon fit somewhere between a decent citizen and a mutant rat. He was six foot three inches tall and weighed upwards of 250 pounds. How he'd managed to get down a chimney, even with the bacon grease, was a miracle. The fact that he'd made it half a block with his pockets jammed full of money and jewelry and his clothes soaked in bacon grease put him in the realm of folk hero on K Street. He was forty-three years old, single, and according to his bond agreement he lived with his mother, Eula.

"His mistake was using bacon grease," Lula said. "First off, it's a waste of good grease when there's other things not so tasty. If he'd greased himself up with motor oil, the dogs wouldn't have tracked him down. 'Course the grease was there for the taking on account of he worked the grill at Mike's Burger Place on K and

Main. They collect bacon grease by the barrel from their bacon burgers."

Lula cruised down K Street and idled across from the three-story redbrick graffiti-riddled building where Billy and his mother lived. We'd been here before, looking for Billy, with no luck.

"Problem is, he's a popular guy," Lula said. "He fried up a good burger, and he was taking care of his momma. I knew his momma from years ago when she was a prime 'ho. Everybody knew she gave one of the best BJs around, but then she got some lip fungus on all her lips, if you know what I mean, and her business kind of fell apart. She was down to doing hand jobs and then she got the arthritis. I hear just about the only thing she can do with her hand now is lift a liquor bottle. Billy said he turned to stealing so he could afford the meds for his momma's fungus. It's kind of noble when you think about it."

"It wasn't noble. It was stupid. Now he's going to jail and his mother will have no one. Not to mention I have serious doubts he was stealing to pay for meds. Last time he got busted he said he'd hijacked twenty cases of Jack Daniel's because he needed to cauterize a bite he got from a rabid dog."

"Twenty cases sounds excessive," Lula said.

The front door to the brick building opened, and Billy Bacon walked out.

"Holy cats," Lula said. "That's Billy Bacon. It's like he was waiting for us to come along and arrest him."

Billy Bacon spotted us in the car and took off at a run up the sidewalk.

"He moves pretty good for a big man," Lula said, "but he don't move as fast as my Firebird."

She gave the Firebird some gas, and just as the car jumped forward Billy Bacon attempted to cross the street. *Whump!* Lula punted Billy Bacon about twenty feet.

"Oops," Lula said.

We got out and looked down at Billy Bacon.

"Are you okay?" Lula asked him.

"I don't know," he said. "I feel dazed. You hit me with your car."

"You were born dazed," Lula said. "And you better hope you didn't put a scratch in my Firebird. I just had it detailed."

Billy Bacon lurched to his feet and looked himself over. "I might have a skinned knee or something. You got insurance?"

"What we got is a pair of handcuffs," Lula said.

I went to cuff him, and he swatted me away. "I don't want to go to jail. I got things to do."

"Like what?" Lula asked him.

"Like lunch."

"We're going for lunch soon as we get you trussed up," Lula said. "We're going for egg salad."

"I might go with you if you buy me a sandwich," Bacon said. "I want ham and cheese. And I want a bag of chips. And not the little bag neither."

I cuffed him and got him settled into the backseat, and Lula drove us the two blocks to the deli.

"I want a egg salad sandwich on worthless white bread," Lula said. "Make sure they pile on lots of egg

35

salad. And then I want a tub of their potato salad, and a tub of their macaroni salad. And I'll take a large Diet Coke."

I left Lula parked at the curb, ran into the deli, and put my order in. Five minutes later I came out and Lula was gone. I looked up and down the street. No Lula. I called her cellphone. No Lula.

Crap.

I waited five minutes and called Lula's cell again. Nothing. I called Ranger and told him Lula had disappeared with my FTA, and I needed a ride.

"Babe," Ranger said. And he hung up.

Ten minutes later Ranger's shiny black Porsche 911 Turbo rolled to a stop in front of the deli. Ranger can't be bothered with anything as trivial as matching his clothes, so he only wears black. Today he was in the standard Rangeman uniform of black shirt with logo and black cargo pants. His skin is flawless, his hair is soft and sexy and cut short, his body is hard muscle and perfect, his eyes are dark brown and unreadable. His past is murky, and he's made it known that his future doesn't involve marriage. It's the present that worries me, because I get damp when I sit next to him, and damp with Ranger isn't good. Damp could turn into a flash flood. I know this for a fact. It's happened. Unfortunately it's *wowie kazowie!* at the moment of liftoff and disaster the day after.

I find it hard to emotionally disentangle after we've been romantic. I suspect Ranger doesn't have this problem. I think I might fall into the category of *pet* for

Ranger. He's fond of me. He's protective. I amuse him. Beyond that, I'm not sure.

I slid onto the passenger seat, put the bag of food on the floor, and buckled myself in.

"I'm worried about Lula. She's not answering her phone. We had Billy Bacon cuffed and sitting in the backseat, and I went into the deli for food. When I came out she was gone."

Ranger glanced down at the bag. "I think we can safely assume she didn't leave voluntarily, since you have the food. I can't see Lula walking away from lunch."

"Maybe you could have your guys keep their eyes open for her."

Ranger provides high-end, specialized security to individuals and businesses willing to pay his price. Rangeman cars are in constant motion around town, checking on accounts, responding to service calls, always plugged into the command center at the Rangeman building.

Ranger called in the request to look for Lula, and we parked across from Billy Bacon's building. We watched the street. No Lula. No Billy Bacon.

"Stay here," Ranger said. "I'll check inside."

Ten minutes later Ranger reappeared and walked to the car.

"Well?" I asked.

"They aren't in there. I spoke to the super, walked through four apartments, and talked to your FTA's mother. I'll spare you the details."

"Was his mother helpful?"

"His mother was passed out on the couch."

I opened the deli bag, took out the turkey club I'd gotten for myself, and gave half to Ranger.

"Billy's never been an especially violent guy," Ranger said. "Maybe he took off with Lula to have a nooner."

I couldn't see Lula choosing sex over egg salad, but I suppose it was possible. I tried her phone again. No answer.

Ranger finished eating and pulled into traffic. "Let's cruise down to Mike's."

"About tonight," I said. "What sort of date is this?"

"Bodyguard detail for one of my better clients. He and his wife have been getting death threats. I have men watching their house, but they're going out tonight, and I need someone to stay close to the wife."

"Where are they going?"

"Viewing at the funeral home on Hamilton."

"I need the red dress for that?"

"The red dress is for me," Ranger said. "I like the red dress."

Mike's Burger Place was a single-room diner with a couple scarred wood tables and some rickety chairs. It smelled like a bacon burger, and I could feel the grease in the air coating my skin, soaking into my hair. No customers. It wasn't a lunch place. It would be packed at five o'clock with people getting takeout. A skinny sick-looking guy stood behind the counter. His white T-shirt was stained with God-knows-what, and he had a spatula in his hand.

"What can I get you?" he asked.

"Information," Ranger said. "I'm looking for Billy."

"Yeah, me too," the guy said. "I'm filling in two shifts on this crap job because Billy took off."

"Do you know where he is?" Ranger asked.

"No. Don't care. What I know is he isn't *here*."

We got outside, and I put my fingertip to the pimple. It felt like it was growing, feeding on the grease.

"Babe," Ranger said.

Babe means many things from Ranger. This was the first time it was a comment on a pimple.

I blew out a sigh. "I'm under a lot of stress."

Ranger's mouth curved into the hint of a smile.

"No, I don't need help relieving my stress," I said to him.

He opened the passenger side door for me. "I'll drive past Lula's house on the way to the bonds office, and I'll have my men do tours down K Street."

"Thanks."

"Have you called the office to see if she's there?"

"I called Connie while you were in the apartment building. Connie hasn't heard from her."

"She hasn't been gone very long."

"I know, but she left without her egg salad," I said to Ranger. "Lula might abandon me, but she'd never drive off without her lunch."

"Maybe something better came along."

CHAPTER
FIVE

Connie was on the phone when I walked into the office. She hung up and looked over at me. "Have you heard from Lula?"

"No." I put the deli bag on Connie's desk. "It's like she vanished into thin air. Left without her lunch."

Vinnie stuck his head out of his inner office. "Do I smell egg salad?"

"It's Lula's lunch," I said.

"So where's Lula?" he asked.

Connie and I did a shoulder shrug.

"Don't know," I said.

Vinnie is like a cartoon character of a bail bondsman. Slicked-back hair, body like a weasel's, pointy-toed shoes, skinny pants, and shiny shirts. He keeps a vodka bottle in his bottom desk drawer, next to his gun.

"Where'd you get the egg salad?" he asked.

"The deli on K Street."

Vinnie ventured out of his office far enough to look in the lunch bag.

"Is this potato salad?" he asked.

"Yeah, and macaroni."

"Anybody want any of this?"

"Not me," Connie said.

"Nope," I said. "Me either."

"Hello, lunch," Vinnie said, and he took the bag into his office and closed and locked his door.

"Any luck with Globovic?" Connie asked.

"I'm going back this afternoon to talk to his girlfriend."

Vinnie yelled from inside his office. "Where's my dessert? There's no dessert here."

"How do you keep from shooting him?" I asked Connie.

"I embezzle money from his bank account. It's pretty satisfying."

When most people say things like that it's a joke. I suspected Connie was serious. And I'm sure she deserves whatever she steals.

"I'm going back to Kiltman," I said. "Let me know if you hear from Lula."

It took three tries to get my car to crank over, but I finally chugged down the street. I watched for the red Firebird as I drove across town. I tried to convince myself that Lula was at a shoe sale or all-you-can-eat sausage bar, but I wasn't having a lot of success. There was a knot in my stomach and a hollow feeling in my chest.

I parked in a lot attached to the student center and walked to the front entrance. It was a big building containing a small theater, a food court, a gallery for student art, and a bunch of offices. The student paper was located in one of the second-floor office spaces. Every inch of the room was cluttered with stacks of papers, office machines, some utilitarian desks, and mismatched chairs. Two women were at a desk, studying something on a laptop.

"Julie Ruley?" I asked.

"That's me," one of the women said.

Julie Ruley was about five four with straight blond hair parted in the middle and tucked back behind her ears. No makeup. Oversized T-shirt. Jeans. Ratty sneakers. Glossy black polish on nails cut short. Hard to tell if she was Malibu Barbie under the T-shirt, and I didn't see any tattoos.

"Would it be possible to speak to you in private?" I asked her.

"Sure," she said, rising out of her chair. "We can talk in the hall."

I found a quiet spot against the wall and introduced myself.

"It's all bogus," Julie said. "Mintner is out to close Zeta, and he's using Gobbles to do it. Mintner asked Gobbles to stop by his house, and when Gobbles got there Mintner was nuts. Gobbles said Mintner was yelling about the evil stuff going on at Zeta. Totally out of control."

"What about the baseball bat?"

"Gobbles was on his way home from playing ball with some friends. He had a bat and a mitt with him."

"That's not the way the police report reads. Mintner said his living room was trashed and Gobbles broke his arm."

"Gobbles said Mintner was on a rant and fell over the ottoman. Maybe that's how his arm got broken. Gobbles left after Mintner fell. I believe Gobbles," Julie said. "He's never lied to me. And I don't like Dean Mintner. No one likes him."

"Why is Gobbles in hiding? Why didn't he show up for his court date?"

"He thinks everything is stacked against him. And I think he's right. People are going to believe Dean Mintner."

"Still, he should check in with the court. We can get him bonded out again. Right now he's considered a felon, and that's not a good thing."

"I'll pass it along if I hear from him."

I gave her my card, and returned to my car. There was a note under the windshield wiper.

Stop hunting Gobbles or else.
P.S. Zeta rules!!

I looked around, but I didn't see anyone I recognized from the fraternity. No one seemed to be watching me. No big deal, I thought. I'd been threatened by psychopathic serial killers, mutant gangbangers, and Morelli's crazy Sicilian grandmother. This hardly registered on my fright meter.

I settled myself behind the wheel, and texted Connie and asked her to get me information on Julie Ruley. With any luck she lived off campus and was harboring Gobbles.

I hadn't heard anything from Ranger or Connie about Lula, so I called Morelli.

"I'm worried about Lula," I told him. "I went into the deli on K Street for lunch, and when I came out she was gone."

"And?"

"She left without her egg salad."

"I could see where that would be worrisome."

"I'm serious. I had an FTA in the backseat of Lula's Firebird. She's not answering her phone, and she's not at the office. I have Ranger's men looking for her, but they haven't turned up anything. I thought you might keep your eyes open for her."

There was a long moment of silence.

"You called Ranger before me?" Morelli asked.

"I needed a ride."

"Your father drives a cab."

"Jeez Louise. I'm reporting a missing person, okay?"

"It hasn't been twenty-four hours since I suggested we back off a little on our relationship and already you're with Ranger."

"I work with the man. I have a professional relationship with him."

"I love you, but you give me acid reflux," Morelli said.

"Yeah, well, you gave me a pimple."

"Really?"

"Yes."

Morelli gave a bark of laughter. "I'll pass the word on Lula. Let me know if she turns up."

I *thunked* my forehead on the steering wheel. My life was a mess. A car drove by, and someone in the backseat threw an egg at me and yelled "Zeta!" It splattered against my driver's side window and oozed down into the door. I looked at my watch and wondered if it was too early to start drinking. A glass of wine or a beer. Just one. Maybe two at the most. Reality check. I'm not good at drinking. I get very happy and then I fall asleep. Since I had to work with Ranger that night, I thought I should delay drinking. Donuts would be a better way to go. A dozen donuts would significantly improve my day.

I hit a Dunkin' Donuts drive-thru and started working on the donuts in the parking lot. By the time I got home there were six left in the box, and I didn't want to see another donut ever again. Not ever. Perhaps a Boston Kreme, but that was it.

I live in a modest apartment building on the fringe of Trenton proper. It's ten minutes from the bonds office, ten minutes from my parents' house, and fifty years out of date. It's a solid three-story building with cheap aluminum windows and an unreliable elevator. My second-floor apartment looks out at the parking lot at the rear of the building. Not exactly scenic, but I have a front-row seat for the occasional dumpster fire.

I was feeling sick from the donuts so I took the stairs, thinking exercise would help. I let myself into my apartment, dropped a morsel of a maple glazed into Rex's cage, and set the rest of the donuts on the counter. Rex rushed over to the piece of donut, stuffed it into his cheek, and hustled it back to his soup can home.

I have a very small area when you first enter my apartment that I like to call my foyer, but probably that's too grand a name for the space. I have a small, practical kitchen, a living room that sort of combines with my dining room, a bedroom, and a retro bath.

45

Retro is another way of saying that my bathroom is really old and ugly.

My dining room serves as my office. I'd inherited the table and chairs from a distant relative. No one else in the family had wanted them. They were nothing I would intentionally buy, but for free they were fine. Rectangular table. Six chairs. Brown wood.

I'm not any kind of cook, and I eat most of my meals standing over the sink, so using the table as a desk wasn't a hardship. I sat down, opened my laptop, and downloaded the new file from Connie.

Julie Ruley was in her senior year at Kiltman. Her parents were divorced. One brother, two years younger. He was enrolled at Penn State. Her mother and stepfather live in South River. Julie's current local address was 2121 Banyan Street. Connie had a side note informing me that this was not on campus.

I checked Banyan out on Google Maps and saw that it was within walking distance of the school. The aerial view told me 2121 Banyan was a large house in a residential neighborhood. Most likely subdivided into student apartments.

Morelli called my cellphone.

"Lula turned up," he said.

"Is she okay?"

"She's okay, but the people she was with are a *mess*. The story I have is that she was at the curb in front of the deli and two idiots got in with guns drawn and told her to drive. Turns out they'd just robbed the Korean grocery two doors down from the deli. I guess they thought Lula's Firebird was a step up from the stolen Kia they'd been driving."

"Where did they take her?"

"Chop shop in Camden."

"Uh-oh."

"Yep. Big mistake. Originally it seems these morons just wanted to get away. The plan had been to acquire enough money to get a bus ticket to Texas, where they'd steal enough money to buy themselves a car wash. They told Lula to take them to the Camden bus station, but then they got to thinking they could make more on the Firebird than they stole from the grocery."

"Lula loves her Firebird."

"That's an understatement. I'm not sure how she managed it, but when they got to Camden and ordered her out of the car, she disarmed the guy in the front and beat the crap out of the two of them. They were happy to see the police arrive."

"Why Camden?"

"They didn't want to leave from Trenton. Too easy to track."

"Brilliant."

"Yeah," Morelli said.

"Where is she now?" I asked.

"I'm not sure. The Camden police released her about an hour ago."

"The FTA? Billy Bacon?"

"Ran off while Lula was trashing the other two guys." There was a moment of silence. "How's the pimple?" he finally asked.

"It's holding its own. How's the heartburn?"

"Not good."

It was almost five o'clock when I opened my door to Lula. She was minus the pink angora sweater, her poison green tank top was smudged, and her hair was less than perfect.

"You're not gonna believe my day," Lula said. "Where's my egg salad?"

"Vinnie ate it."

"Say what?"

"I was worried about you when you disappeared. Why didn't you call?"

"I got kidnapped and one of the idiots took my cellphone. What do you mean Vinnie ate my egg salad?"

"I brought the stuff from the deli back to the office and Vinnie ate it."

"He got some nerve. I was looking forward to that egg salad."

"We can get more tomorrow."

Lula's attention moved to the box on the counter. "Is that donuts I see?"

"Help yourself."

Lula took a jelly donut. "I'm about starved. First off I got kidnapped and they wanted to go to Camden." She shook her head. "Camden. Like I haven't anything better to do than to drive to Camden. And then when we got to Camden they said I should get out and walk home on account of they were taking my Firebird to a chop shop. Okay, I get that they need money to start up a business. Not that I'm saying it's the right thing to do

48

or anything. But you don't take a acetylene torch to a red Firebird. It's not done. And I just had it detailed."

"Morelli said you trashed them."

"I might have got carried away in the moment. It's the protective nature in me needing to protect my Firebird."

Lula finished the jelly donut and took a chocolate covered.

"And Billy Bacon got away?" I asked her.

"Yup. He took advantage of the situation and ran like a rabbit, handcuffs and all. I drove around looking for him after the police got done talking to me, but I couldn't find him. So what did you do with the rest of the day? Did you find Globovic?"

"I talked to his girlfriend. I'm sure she knows where he is. I might go back with Ranger tonight and look around."

"Sounds like a plan to me. You mind if I take the rest of these donuts home?"

"They're yours."

CHAPTER
SIX

For the viewing I settled on skinny black slacks, a dressy white T-shirt with a scoop neck, and a fitted short red jacket. The outfit had the advantage of looking good with black ballet flats, which would be excellent for chasing down a killer if the occasion arose. I had my gun in my purse, but I hadn't been able to find any bullets. With any luck, Ranger would never know about the bullets.

I was downstairs waiting at seven o'clock when Ranger pulled up in a black Porsche Cayenne. It was his personal fleet car. Very luxe but equipped with ankle restraints bolted onto the backseat floor in case he had to transport a bad guy.

"Babe," Ranger said as I slid in next to him. "Didn't want to risk the red dress?"

"Mrs Kranski and Mrs Rundig will most likely be at this viewing. They would call my mother and tell her I was at the viewing wearing a tight red dress with cleavage, and then my mother would head straight for the Jim Beam bottle. Bad enough that I'm going to be there with you. That's worth two Advil."

"I thought your mother liked me."

"My grandmother likes you. My mother worries that you might be related to Satan."

The funeral home is on the edge of the Burg, short for Chambersburg. Originally the Burg was a mob enclave, but most of the mob has now moved on to classier neighborhoods. The factory workers, bus drivers, plumbers, cops, and government worker bees remain. I grew up in the Burg, and my parents still live there. Houses are modest. Bars are plentiful. Crime is low. Gossip is rampant. The funeral home is the Burg equivalent to a country club. It's free entertainment for everyone but the immediate family of the deceased.

People in the Burg go to viewings for the cookies, not for the dead guy in Slumber Room No. 2. The building was originally a large Victorian-style home with a wraparound porch. Thirty years ago it was sold to the Stiva family and converted into a mortuary. It's since changed hands, but people still refer to it as *Stiva's.*

We drove to the funeral home and Ranger parked in a space reserved for him.

"Who's the deceased?" I asked.

"Harry Getz. Someone drilled two holes in him. Looks like it happened when he opened his front door to someone. Initially it went down as armed robbery, but nothing was stolen, and Getz had a lot of enemies. I think Morelli is the principal on it. We'll be providing security for Harry's business partner, Doug Linken, and his wife, Monica."

"Hard feelings with the family?"

"Hard feelings with everyone. Getz and Linken owned a construction business, G&L Builds. Mostly commercial properties. Strip malls. And they had some smaller businesses that were associated with the construction. G&L Builds overextended and imploded. There was a lot of ugly finger-pointing and name-calling, and it's going through a contentious bankruptcy. A lot of people are going to get shortchanged."

We walked to the front of the building. A black Rangeman SUV pulled up, and the Linkens got out. Ranger introduced me, and we all walked into the funeral home together.

Doug Linken was a nice-looking man in his early sixties. He was wearing a dark gray suit, white shirt, and gray and black striped tie. Monica Linken looked younger than her husband, but she'd probably had work done, so it was hard to tell her age. And she looked like she spent time at the gym. Blond hair pulled back at the nape of her neck. Simple black suit. Massive diamond studs in her ears. Bright red lipstick. I thought if she hocked the earrings she might be able to get the business back on its feet.

There were three slumber rooms occupied. Harry Getz had the place of honor in Slumber Room No. 1. It was the largest viewing room and got awarded to the newly departed who was expected to draw the biggest crowd. A controversial murder would only be trumped by a decapitation or fraternal lodge Grand Bigwig, and there were currently neither of those in residence.

The lobby was filled with the usual freeloaders and gawkers. My Grandma Mazur was one of them. A hush fell over the crowd when we entered, and they parted,

52

like when Moses showed up at the Red Sea, to let us make our way to the viewing. Ranger and I were known in the community, and it was obvious we were there to ensure the Linkens' safety.

Grandma Mazur spotted me from across the room. "Yoo-hoo!" she called. And she waved.

Grandma has some things in common with the Queen of England. They have the same hairstyle, they each carry their purse in the crook of their arm, and no one tells either of them what to do.

Grandma was wearing a sleeveless dress with big red and pink flowers on it. Her lipstick was a bright pink to match the flowers on the dress. Her shoes and her purse were black patent leather. The purse was big enough to hold her .45 long barrel.

The double doors were open to the viewing room, and I could see that every chair was occupied. A line of condolence wishers snaked from the casket almost to the double doors. Usually viewings at Stiva's are a respite from mourning, with a lot of gossip and laughter and boozing it up. But the atmosphere in Slumber Room No. 1 was sullen tonight. Doug and Monica took their place at the end of the line, and a buzz went through the room. Heads turned and eyes focused on the Linkens, and the climate of the room ratcheted up from sullen to hostile.

Ranger leaned close, and I caught a hint of the scent of the shower gel that always lingers on his skin, and I could feel the warmth from his body.

"Going to be a long night," he whispered, his lips brushing against my ear.

I got a rush that went all the way down to my toes. Okay, so I know it wasn't a sexy message, but jeez Louise, the man was fine.

We inched our way forward, and as we got closer to the deceased I could see the immediate family glaring at the Linkens.

"What's with all the animosity?" I asked Ranger.

"I'll spare you the complicated financials, but Doug Linken will benefit from his partner's death. The Getz family will not."

Grandma Mazur elbowed her way through the crowd and sidled up to me.

"Isn't this a pip of a viewing?" she said. "Standing room only. Take a close look at his neck when you get up there. If you look real good you can see the marks from where he got shot. That's not something you see every day."

"Look over there," I said to Grandma. "A seat just opened up in the second row."

"I'm on it," Grandma said, rushing to the empty seat.

"She likes when she can be up close," I said to Ranger.

Ranger looked over at Grandma. "That's a lot to live up to, Babe."

A woman in a pink suit and a man in a tweedy sport coat stood at the casket. I guessed they were the wife and brother. Ranger stepped in front of the Linkens as they approached the casket. I remained behind, so we had them sandwiched between us.

54

"Our condolences," Doug Linken said to the family, not sounding all that sincere.

"You have a lot of nerve showing up here," the brother said. "You swindled him, and you swindled us. And don't think you have us fooled. You killed him. You killed him."

"*Killer!*" the woman shrieked at Linken. "*Dirty, rotten killer!*"

Ranger put himself between the Linkens and the Getz family and moved the Linkens toward the side door that led to the back exit.

"Not so fast," Monica Linken said. "I want a cookie."

"I'll have my men stop at a bakery," Ranger said.

"I don't want a bakery cookie. I want a cookie from the lobby," Monica said. "And I'm not leaving out of the side door like we're criminals or something."

"Well, I'm leaving out the side door," Doug Linken said. "Those people are nuts."

"Escort Mrs Linken to the cookie table," Ranger said to me. "The car will be waiting for her at the front door."

I followed Monica as she slowly made her way through the crush of people. Grandma was out of her seat and was half a step behind me.

"Don't worry," Grandma said. "I've got your back."

"Not necessary," I said to Grandma. "We're just going for cookies."

"Me too," Grandma said. "I hope they got some of them vanilla sandwich cookies left, but if anything goes down I'm ready to rock and roll."

We reached the cookie table and Monica poured herself a cup of tea and took an oatmeal raisin coolde.

"I could put your tea in a to-go cup," I said to Monica.

"I'm in no rush," Monica said. "So just chill."

Grandma Mazur snagged the last vanilla sandwich cookie and turned to Monica. "What's the story?" Grandma asked Monica. "Did your husband kill Harry?"

"Excuse me?" Monica said. "*Who are you?*"

"I'm Stephanie's granny," Grandma said.

Monica looked at me. "You brought your grandmother? What kind of an agency does my husband employ?"

"I didn't bring her," I said. "She was already here. She goes to all the viewings."

"Not *all* of them," Grandma said. "Sometimes they conflict with my television shows."

I could see people jostling around by the viewing room door. Voices were raised. There was a disturbance of some sort, and I didn't want to hang around to identify the source.

"We should go," I said to Monica. "*Now.*"

Monica pretended not to hear. She reached for another cookie, and Harry's wife knocked me aside and got into Monica's face.

"No cookies for killers," the woman said to Monica. "I paid for these cookies and you can't have any."

The wife slapped the cookie out of Monica's hand, and Monica splashed her tea onto the widow's pink suit.

"Bitch!" the wife yelled. "You cow. You cheap whore."

In an instant they were on the ground, gouging eyes and pulling hair. I tried to wade in to separate them, but they were rolling around and I couldn't get a grip. Someone kicked out and caught me in the back of the leg, and I went down too. The funeral director ran in, made the mistake of getting too close, and Monica bit him.

There was a deafening *bang!* and everyone froze. A chunk of plaster fell out of the ceiling and smashed onto the floor.

"What the heck?" the funeral director asked.

"Edna shot up the ceiling again," Mabel Schein said.

"I figured someone had to get their attention," Grandma said.

Ranger stepped out of the mob, scooped Monica up, and whisked her through the lobby and out the door. I got to my feet and helped Grandma fit her six-shooter back into her purse.

"This was worth the price of admission," Grandma said.

"Do you need a ride home?"

"No. I came with Betty Shatz. We're going to the diner for rice pudding after this."

CHAPTER
SEVEN

The Rangeman SUV was pulling away with the
Linkens inside when I approached Ranger.

"Another job well done," I said.

"I assume they were fighting over cookies."

"More or less. The best part was when Monica
Linken bit the funeral director."

"I'm sorry I missed that."

"I need to check out an address tonight. I'm looking
for a Kiltman student, and I think he might be hiding
out with his girlfriend. Want to come along?"

He gave me a long slow look from my head to my
toes, and I figured he was wondering how difficult it
would be to get me out of the skinny slacks.

"Don't even think about it," I said.

A hint of a smile curved the corners of his mouth,
and he wrapped an arm around me. "Babe."

We walked to his Porsche, buckled up, and drove
across town. It was dark by the time we got to Banyan
Street. We sat across from 2121 for a while, watching
the house.

"Do you have an apartment number?" Ranger asked.

"2B."

"So she's most likely on the second floor. Lights are on in the front. Let's get out and take a look at the back."

It was a large house, probably built in the fifties for a big family. The lot was relatively small. The details were lost in deep shadow. A driveway hugged one side and led to a four-car garage on the back edge of the property. No one out and about but Ranger and me. Lights were also on in back windows. No shades were drawn, but we couldn't see anyone moving around.

"What do these people look like?" Ranger asked.

"Julie Ruley is about five foot four, shoulder-length blond hair, nice looking in a back-to-nature kind of way. Ken Globovic has sandy blond hair. A little pudgy. File says he's five ten. His mug shot made him look like Christopher Robin."

Ranger was wearing a perfectly tailored black suit, black cross-trainers, a black Glock, and a dressy black T-shirt. He handed me his suit jacket, ran a couple steps at the building, went up the side like Spider-Man, and did an effortless, silent pull-up onto the slanted roof that covered the wraparound porch. He moved from one window to the next, and disappeared around the side of the house. Minutes later he returned and quietly swung down from the roof.

"I saw a woman who matched your description of Julie Ruley," he said. "I didn't see a man in the apartment. And I didn't see anything that would lead me to believe a man was living there."

"No underwear on the floor, dirty dishes stacked up in the sink, porno magazines lying around?"

"Only hers."

We walked back to his car and sat there for a while. Nothing happened.

"This is boring," I said.

Ranger looked over at me. "I could fix that."

"Tempting, but no."

"Do you have any other leads on him?"

"He's a big deal in his fraternity. I'm not sure he would chance going there. He's a biology major, but I can't see him hiding out in the bio lab. Supposedly he's been seen on campus late at night."

"Family?"

"Not local."

"Friends?"

"Tons."

"You look young enough to be a college student. Maybe you should go undercover and get cozy with the fraternity brothers."

"Too late. They've already seen me."

"So what's your plan?"

"I thought I'd sit here until I needed a bathroom."

"Is that going to happen anytime soon?"

"Hard to say."

This wasn't the first time I'd been on a stakeout with Ranger. Ranger has infinite patience. He goes into a zone, his heart rate slows, and you have to hold a mirror under his nose to see if he's breathing. He can sit like this for hours, stalking his prey. On the other hand, I have *no* patience. I'm not the queen of the stakeout. After I've checked my email on my phone I have nothing.

60

Ranger tugged at my ponytail. "How about a burger and fries? Are you hungry?"

"Yes!"

We went to a small dark bar four blocks away and settled into a corner booth. It was far enough from Kiltman that it wasn't frequented by college kids. There were some people at the bar who looked like regulars, and there was another couple in a booth on the other side of the room.

We ordered burgers, French fries, and onion rings. Ranger is former Special Forces, and he's maintained his Special Forces level of fitness. He works out. He has only an occasional glass of beer or wine. He eats healthy. When our food was set on the table he removed the bun from his burger and took a single French fry for a test drive. I removed the lettuce and tomato from my burger, saturated the fries with ketchup, and ate all the onion rings.

A guy at the bar stood and walked toward us on his way to the men's room. My heart skipped a beat when he got close. I was almost positive it was Gobbles.

"Ken?" I asked him. "Ken Globovic?"

He looked at me, and he looked at Ranger, and he looked at me again. His first reaction was confusion, and then panic.

"Um, no," he said.

Ranger reached out for him, and Globovic jumped away and took off. Ranger and I were out of the booth and on our feet, but Gobbles had a head start. He ran into the narrow galley kitchen, knocked over a cart filled with glasses, and ran out the back door. By the time we maneuvered around the cart, Gobbles was gone, disappeared into the night.

Two line cooks watched the whole thing with wide eyes and open mouths. Ranger apologized in Spanish, and we returned to our booth. Ranger dropped some money on the table, and we left. We drove the neighborhood, covering it in a grid pattern, but didn't see Gobbles.

"At least we know he's not in Argentina," I said to Ranger.

"Have Connie run a check on the fraternity brothers tomorrow, and see if anyone is renting near the bar."

"Instinct tells you he isn't living with Julie Ruley?"

"I'm sure he has contact with her, but I doubt he'd be having his dinner in a bar that was four blocks away if he was living with her. He'd be in her apartment eating takeout pizza."

Personally I thought she looked more like lentils and quinoa, and that could be why Gobbles was in a bar. Ranger might not understand that, since lentils and quinoa would be a step up from the tree bark and desert beetles he probably ate when he was in Special Forces.

It was almost eleven o'clock when Ranger parked in the lot behind my apartment building. He walked me into the small deserted lobby, drew me close against him, and kissed me. The kiss was light at first and then got serious. I felt my fingers curl into his shirt and someone moaned. It might have been me. Ranger pushed the elevator button, the doors opened, and he moved us into the elevator. By the time we got to my apartment door I was thinking he needed to come in to make sure everything was secure. Check under the bed to get rid of any serial rapists or scary, drooly monsters. And while he was checking under the bed I might have to get undressed because I was having a massive hot flash.

We were in the middle of the living room, halfway to the bedroom, when Ranger's phone rang. He took his hand out from under my shirt, answered his phone, and stared at the floor while he listened. He asked "When?" and "Where?" He disconnected.

"That was Tank," Ranger said. "Someone shot Doug Linken."

"How bad is it?"

"He's in surgery. Tank said it doesn't look good. He said the wife looks even worse."

"She was shot too?"

"No. She's hysterical." Ranger grabbed my hand and tugged me to the door. "I need you at the hospital."

I dug my feet in. "No way. You want me to babysit Monica Linken."

"Yeah. I'll pay you time and a half."

"Not enough."

He stood hands on hips, looking at me. "I'll give you a car."

"Permanently? Will it be mine or will it be temporary?"

"It'll be yours until you trash it. Considering your record with cars you won't have it long."

"Okay. I'll do it."

It wasn't such a great deal. Ranger gave me cars all the time. Sooner or later he got fed up with me driving around in a hunk of junk, and he gave me a car.

At this time of night, when there wasn't much traffic, it was a short trip to St. Francis Hospital. The hospital was on Hamilton, a couple blocks from the bonds office, on the edge of the Burg. If you needed complicated brain surgery, it was best not to go to St. Francis. If you had a gunshot wound, you were in the right place. Trenton saw a fair amount of shooting. The surgeons at St. Francis had a lot of practice removing bullets.

Ranger swung into the emergency room drop-off, and we were met by a uniformed Rangeman guy. He gave us directions to Monica Linken, and he took the car. Rangeman valet service.

Monica had been placed in a small waiting room reserved for families of surgery patients. Hal, one of Ranger's security force, was standing guard at the door. He looked like he wanted to hurl himself out a fourth-floor window. Monica was inside, pacing and sucking on an electronic cigarette. She spotted Ranger and rushed at him.

"You're supposed to be protecting us," she yelled. "Is this protecting us?"

"We weren't hired for twenty-four-hour continuous personal protection," Ranger said. Very calm. No emotion. "The alarm system in your house is working perfectly. Your outdoor perimeter security lights are working perfectly."

"They were working so perfectly they got my stupid husband shot. He walked outside to sneak a smoke, the lights went on, and *bang!*, some asshole shot him. He was an easy target."

"Unfortunate," Ranger said. "Do you have any idea who did this?"

"There's a big list. He wasn't popular. Hell, I didn't even like him. And I didn't see anything, if that's what you mean. I was watching television. One of the *CSI* shows. There was lots of shooting. I didn't even find him until there was a commercial. I went to the kitchen and the back door was open. And there he was. Facedown on the patio in lots of blood." Monica took a massive drag on her fake cigarette. "I'm never going to get the blood out of that stone. I'm going to have to replace it. Do you have any idea how expensive that is? Bastard rip-off stonemasons."

"I'm going to check on your husband," Ranger said to Monica. "Stephanie will stay with you."

"Great," Monica said. "That makes me feel a lot better. Not at all. How about her crazy grandmother? Is she here too?"

"Just me," I told Monica.

She sucked on her e-cigarette. some more and watched Ranger leave. "Nice ass," she said. "Is he boinking you?"

"Not recently," I said. "I sort of have a boyfriend. At least I thought I did."

"Yeah, I sort of have a husband, but that wouldn't stop me."

"Looks like you're trying to quit smoking?"

"I swear if you really enjoy something you can count on it being no good for you. We switched to these electronic things a couple weeks ago. I'm not happy, but I'm managing to stick with the program. Doug cheated a lot. He cheated a lot with everything. Between you and me, I wouldn't mind if smoking killed him, if you know what I mean."

Jeez Louise this was freaking depressing. This was way beyond a Jeep. This was worth a Mercedes or a Porsche.

"I need a drink," Monica said. "Send one of those Rangeman guys out for some booze. Vodka would be good. I'm ready to drink it straight up from the bottle. Cripes, just get me a straw."

"Gee, I'd love to do that for you, but they only take orders from Ranger."

"Then go get Hot Stuff and tell him I need a drink."

I called Ranger and told him Monica needed vodka.

"She's going to need more than vodka," Ranger said. "She's going to need Slumber Room No. 1. Her husband didn't make it. The doctor is on his way to talk to her."

"So about that vodka?"

"I'll send Hal out for it."

I disconnected and put my phone back in my purse. "Hal's going for vodka," I told her.

"Thank God. Why do they make these rooms so bleak? I mean, look at the television they've got here. It's from 1970."

I thought it looked a lot like the television I had in my apartment. I checked my watch. I was counting down minutes until the vodka arrived.

A tired-looking man in blue scrubs stuck his head into the room. "Mrs Linken?" he asked. "I'd like to speak with you."

"I'm going to step out for a minute," I said. "I'll stay close if anyone needs me."

Ranger was waiting in the hall.

"Did the Linkens have perimeter security cameras?" I asked him.

"No. They didn't want them."

"Too bad. They might have gotten the shooter on video."

"Doug Linken didn't want some of his visitors caught on camera."

"Shady business partners?"

"Shady sexual encounters," Ranger said.

"So where do we go from here?"

"I'll wait to see if Mrs Linken needs our help, and then we'll go home."

Ten minutes later we had Monica Linken settled into the backseat of a Rangeman SUV. She was chugging vodka out of the bottle, and she was smiling.

"Not exactly a grieving widow," I said to Ranger, watching the car pull away from the curb.

"Hal will get her locked into the house, and then he'll hang out in the driveway overnight. I imagine there's a crime scene crew combing through her backyard. I'll get in touch with her tomorrow to see if she wants us to continue our service."

"Do you think she's in any danger?"

"Yeah. I think she could pass out and never wake up if she drinks that whole bottle of vodka."

CHAPTER
EIGHT

I stepped out of my apartment at eight a.m. and found a Rangeman guy waiting for me in the hall.

"This is for you," he said, handing me a Mercedes key. "The paperwork is in the glove box. Ranger said you would understand."

I took the key and thanked him. Ranger was efficient, as always. We exited the building together, and the Rangeman guy waited for me to find my new car and get behind the wheel before he left.

Ranger had given me a little SUV. I suspected it had originally been a fleet car because it had the ankle restraint loops welded onto the floor of the backseat. It smelled like a new car, and it was immaculately clean.

I drove to the bonds office, parked at the curb, and Lula opened the office door before I got to it.

"Looks to me like Ranger gave you another car," Lula said. "And this one's a Mercedes. You must have done somethin' good to that man."

"Sorry to disappoint you, but no. It was a business deal."

"I do business all the time, and I don't get no Mercedes," Lula said.

Connie looked over at me. "I hear Doug Linken was shot. Was that on your watch?"

"No. They were home. He went outside to smoke and someone shot him."

I saw their eyes shift from me to the front door, and I turned to look. It was Morelli.

"Here comes Officer Hottie," Lula said. "I tell you, I wouldn't mind him putting me in cuffs."

Morelli hung at the door and crooked his finger at me. "I want to talk to you," he said. "Outside."

Crap. Talking to Morelli right now wasn't high on my list of favorite activities. It came right between stick a fork in my eye and drink Drano. I mean, I really like Morelli. Actually, I *love* Morelli, but I had no clue what to say or think at this point beyond wanting to punch him in the face.

"Sorry I didn't call last night," he said. "It was a busy night. Gangbanger drive-by, and then I pulled the Linken shooting."

"Lucky you."

"I had a brief conversation with Mrs Linken last night just before she passed out. She said you and Ranger were supposed to be protecting them."

"We escorted them to the Getz viewing, but then we were off duty. When word went but that Doug Linken was shot, Ranger wanted me at the hospital to babysit Monica."

"Did she need babysitting?"

"Mostly she needed vodka."

"Did you get anything useful out of her?"

"Her big news was that she didn't have the perfect marriage, and Doug had a lot of enemies. Do you think she could have shot him?"

"It's doubtful. It looks like the shooter was twenty to thirty feet away, shooting toward the house."

"Monica said she didn't pay attention to the gunshots because she was watching *CSI* and there was a lot of shooting. I find that hard to believe, but maybe it's possible. She went to the kitchen during a commercial and noticed the door was open."

"The first responders said it looked like Doug Linken went out to smoke."

"Monica said the same thing. They were trying to quit, but Doug wasn't having total luck with it."

"So that problem's solved for him," Morelli said. "It's too early for me to disturb the widow with questions. Would you like to go for coffee?"

"No! I think you're a jerk."

"I come by it honestly. It runs in my family."

This is true. All the men in Morelli's family have been losers. All except Morelli. Somewhere in his twenties he'd managed to grow up. He was a really good cop, and until two days ago he'd been an okay boyfriend.

"I can't believe you're thinking about a job change. I thought you loved being a cop."

"I've got acid reflux."

"I thought that was from *me*."

"Yeah, you too." His cellphone buzzed and he checked the text message. "I have to go. They're doing the autopsy on Linken first thing this morning, and I want to attend."

"Maybe *that's* why you have acid reflux."

"Dead people don't bother me. I worry about the living. Lately I'm thinking this planet is just a videogame designed to amuse an alien race with a sick sense of humor."

"Jeez."

Morelli pulled me close and kissed me with a lot of tongue. "Stay safe," he said, releasing me, heading for his green SUV.

He'd gotten the car so he could haul his big orange dog, Bob, around. It wasn't brand-new, but it ran okay, and it looked pretty good except where Bob had gnawed a hole in the backseat. Bob had an eating disorder. Bob ate *everything*.

"Looks like a good day in Plumville," Lula said when I went back inside. "You got a Mercedes from one hot guy and a smokin' hot kiss from another, and it's not even nine o'clock yet. What's Morelli up to this morning that he had to rush off?"

"Doug Linken's autopsy is scheduled," I said. "Morelli's attending."

"That's a fast-track autopsy," Connie said. "Business must be slow at the morgue."

"I spotted Ken Globovic last night, but he got away," I said to Connie. "He was at the corner of M Street and Hawthorne. I was hoping you could run his fraternity brothers through the system and see if anyone is living there."

"There's a bar on that corner that got excellent onion rings," Lula said. "I wouldn't mind taking a personal look around that neighborhood at lunchtime."

"Works for me," I said. "We can do a fast tour through Billy Bacon's hood, hunt down Julie Ruley for a chat, and hopefully by that time Connie will have an address for me that's close to the bar."

Connie pulled a padded envelope off the corner of her desk and handed it to me. "This came in for you yesterday. No return address. Maybe you want to open it outside, just in case."

"That's not funny," Lula said to Connie. "There's crazy people out there that Stephanie put in jail, and now some of them are getting out on parole. Fortunately most of them aren't smart enough to get hold of anthrax or build a bomb. Still, you never know, right?"

I opened the envelope and pulled out a picture of a naked guy. He was in a bathtub and his Mr Happy was floating peacefully in the water.

Lula looked over my shoulder at the picture. "That's a real nice bath caddy he got," she said. "I bet he got that at Pottery Barn."

Connie came around and looked at it. "That's Daniel Craig. I've seen that picture before. It's all over YouTube."

"Get out," Lula said. "Daniel Craig is James Bond. He wouldn't have a limp little wiener floating around like that."

"Is there a note?" Connie asked.

I checked the envelope. "No note. Just the picture signed by someone named Scooter."

I gave the picture back to Connie. "Toss it. I don't know anyone named Scooter."

"I'll take it," Lula said. "I keep a file of future household improvements."

I currently was using a canvas green and tan camouflage messenger bag as a purse. I thought it complemented my jeans, T-shirt, and sneakers, and it was able to hold all the tools of my trade. Files of felons, cuffs, hairspray, lip gloss, stun gun, hair brush, pepper spray, cellphone, pimple concealer, Kleenex, hand sanitizer, car keys, etc. I hiked the bag higher onto my shoulder and turned to leave.

"Text me if you have any luck with the fraternity brothers," I said to Connie.

"I'm on it."

"This here's gonna be good," Lula said. "We get to ride around in your fancy new car."

I drove to Billy Bacon's apartment building, and Lula and I climbed the stairs to the third floor. We knocked twice and no one answered. Lula tried the door. Locked.

"I got drugs," Lula yelled.

Billy Bacon's mother opened the door and looked out at us, and the door across the hall opened and a young guy looked out.

"How much?" he asked.

"I lied," Lula said. "And anyways I wasn't yelling at your door."

Billy Bacon's mother gave a disgusted grunt and slammed the door shut.

"Hey," Lula said, pounding on the door. "Open up. It's Lula, and I need to talk to you."

The door opened and Bacon's mother squinted at us. "I don't know no Lula."

"I was friends with Charlene. You and her used to tag team back when you were a working 'ho."

"Do you got any liquor?"

"Nope," Lula said. "We didn't think to bring any."

"Well, I might talk to you if you had liquor."

I pulled a ten-dollar bill out of my bag and waved it at Bacon's mother. She snatched at it, and I jerked it away.

"Is Billy here?" I asked her.

"Billy who?"

"Your *son*."

"Haven't seen him. He was gone when I got up."

"When did you get up?" Lula asked.

"Just now."

"Would you mind if we look in your apartment?" I asked her.

"Are you gonna give me that ten?"

I gave her the ten, and she stepped aside. The apartment consisted of two rooms. Small bedroom, bathroom, small living room with a refrigerator, two-burner stove, and a sink. There was a tattered couch, a Formica-topped table with two chairs, a television, and a twin-sized mattress with rumpled bedding on the floor in the living room. No Billy Bacon.

I left my card on the table, and Lula and I trudged down the stairs.

"I hate to see how she's fallen on hard times," Lula said. "She used to make good money. She had one of the best corners on Stark Street. She didn't even used to work in the rain. She was a nice-weather 'ho. And now look at her. She got something growing on her lip that you only see in a horror movie."

We sat in the Mercedes and watched the street for a while. No one went in or out of the apartment building. Billy Bacon didn't magically appear.

"Maybe we should check out his former place of employment," Lula said. "He might have gone back to cooking burgers."

I drove to Mike's Burgers and idled at the curb while Lula went in to ask about Billy. She returned with a giant soda and a bucket of fries. No Billy.

"They don't know where he is," Lula said. "They said they think he's hiding on account of some crazy-ass bounty hunter almost got him killed."

"That would be you," I said to Lula.

"I was an innocent bystander. I was minding my own business and I got carjacked. You want some fries?"

"They're green."

"They said it was some special potatoes, and they didn't even charge me extra for it."

"I'll pass."

CHAPTER
NINE

It was midmorning when I got to Kiltman. I parked in a lot behind the administration building and we cut across campus to the Zeta house.

Three women were marching back and forth across the front lawn. They were holding signs that called for the annihilation of the Zetas.

"What's the deal?" Lula asked one of the women. "What's wrong with the Zetas?"

"Everything. They're all pigs. It's a totally sexist fraternity."

"I'm pretty sure fraternities are supposed to be sexist," Lula said to her. "Now, if people started vomiting up cockroaches when they were in there, that would be something. You ever see anything like that?"

"Not cockroaches," one of the women said. "Just normal vomit."

"That makes me feel a lot better," Lula said. "I was worried about the cockroaches."

The front door was open so we walked in. All was quiet. No pigs milling around. No cockroaches that we could see.

"It's a big house," Lula said. "Gobbles could be hiding somewhere here. Are you going to go door to door?"

"No. I don't want to see what's behind some of these doors."

"Evil?"

"Naked men."

"Do you want me to look?" Lula asked.

"Not without cause."

"I think he'd be in the cellar," Lula said. "They're always hiding either in the cellar or the attic. 'Course sometimes they're in a closet or under the bed. And remember that time that little person was in the clothes dryer? Although I don't think he got in there voluntarily since he was getting tumbled and someone had to have pushed the button."

"My experience is that fraternities usually have bars in the cellar. Or at least a cold room for storing kegs of beer."

"Hey," Lula called to a guy who was heading for the front door. "How do we get into the cellar?"

"Cellar's locked. Stuff gets stored there."

"Who has a key to the cellar?" I asked him.

"I don't know. A bunch of people. Gobbles had a key. Professor Pooka has a key."

"Why Professor Pooka?"

"He's our faculty advisor. Some of the fraternities have house mothers, but we got a house dude."

"I guess that's on account of you're sexist," Lula said.

"It's on account of the last house mother enjoyed the parties too much and got pregnant, so we got assigned Pooka."

"Does he live here?" I asked.

"No, but he stops in every day to check on things. What's your deal with the cellar?"

"We're meter readers," Lula said. "We gotta check on the gas and water shit."

"I think the meters are outside. Just walk around the house. I think they're in the back."

"I told her they'd be in the back," Lula said, "but Stephanie here thought they were in the cellar."

Lula and I exited the house and walked around outside.

"There's no windows or doors in the cellar," Lula said. "We've been all around the house and there's no cellar windows."

"I want to check in with Julie Ruley but according to the schedule I have she's in class until eleven."

"That's good because it gives us time to go see Pooka and get the key to the cellar."

"What's with this cellar obsession? It makes no sense that Gobbles would be hiding in the cellar. He doesn't even have a second exit."

"He could have a secret exit. There could be a secret tunnel that goes to the restaurant on M and Hawthorne."

"That's a long tunnel."

"Well, I got a feeling. I'm extra perceptionary that way. I just know things. Sometimes I wake up at night and I think it's gonna rain, and it almost always does."

78

"Amazing."

"Yeah, not everyone's got a talent like that. I could be a weathergirl on television. The hell with Doppler and all that shit. If I say it's gonna rain you could go to the bank with it."

"Okay, I guess it wouldn't hurt to talk to Pooka again. At the very least he should be able to tell us who Gobbles hung with."

We hiked to the science building and took the elevator to the third floor. We shared the elevator with six other women who looked like students. The elevator doors opened at the third floor and the women rushed out and down the hall to the biology lab.

"Guess the wonder kid is at work," Lula said. "I think the *wonder* part is how he gets anything done what with all the women ogling him."

Pooka's office door was closed. I rapped on it and someone yelled, "*Go away!*"

"That sounds like Pooka," Lula said. "Hey, baggy pants," she yelled back. "Open the door."

The door was wrenched open and Pooka glared out at us. "I'm busy."

"How busy could you be in those pajamas?" Lula asked him.

Pooka looked down at his pants. "These aren't pajamas. These are dhoti."

"Doody?"

"*Dhoti*. They're Indian."

"Did the necklace tell you to wear them?" Lula asked.

"The amulet is more effective when my boys can breathe."

"That makes sense," Lula said. "I bet there'd be a lot less aggression in the world if everybody's boys had some breathing room. I mean, how can you be happy when your nuts are all cramped together? One of the Zeta people told us you were the house dude. You ever see anyone vomiting up cockroaches there?"

"No."

"Are you sure?"

"I would have remembered."

"I'm still looking for Ken Globovic," I said to Pooka. "Who were his close friends?"

"I don't know. I have more important things to do than keep track of Globovic's friends."

"Like what?" Lula asked.

"Like *anything. Anything* would be more important than paying attention to Ken Globovic's every move."

"Not to us," Lula said. "We gotta find him or we don't get paid."

"Not my problem," Pooka said. "Get out of my office."

"Nuh-unh," Lula said. "I'm not leaving until you help us find Gobbles."

"I'm calling security," Pooka said.

Lula leaned forward. "You make one move to that phone, and I'm gonna sit on you until you're a grease spot on the floor."

"I have research to do," Pooka said. "You're wasting my valuable time."

"Now we're getting somewhere," Lula said. "What kind of research? Are you working on global warming?"

"No."

"Then your research isn't so important, is it?"

"Global warming is a hoax. It's an example of one more fraud fed to the American people by its corrupt government," Pooka said.

"You shouldn't be talking about the government like that," Lula said. "It's disrespectful. And they might come get you and lock you up."

Pooka stared at Lula. "Have you heard something?"

"Not exactly," Lula said. "It's more I get these premonitions on account of you sound like a nut."

"Brian Karwatt," Pooka said.

"What about him?" I asked.

"Globovic hung out with Brian Karwatt. Now get out of my office."

"Yeah, but I got a premonition about the cellar at the Zeta house," Lula said. "I think Gobbles might be hiding out there."

"He's not," Pooka said. "I was at the house last night and Gobbles wasn't in the cellar."

"He might have slipped in this morning," Lula said. "I've got one of those feelings."

"I told you he's not in the cellar," Pooka said. "End of discussion. Go bother someone else."

"Thank you for your time," I said to Pooka. "We appreciate your help."

He did a stiff-armed gesture at the door. "*Go!*"

"One last thing," Lula said. "Could I touch your power amulet?"

"No!"

I tugged Lula out of the office, into the hall, and Pooka slammed his door shut and locked it.

"He's got issues," Lula said. "I don't think those loose pants are doing anything for him."

"I want to go back to Zeta. I'd like to talk to Brian Karwatt."

"What about Julie Ruley?"

"I know where she lives. I can catch her later."

We crossed the field back to the Zeta house. No one was picketing anymore. A couple guys were lounging on the small second-floor balcony over the front door. There was movement inside on the first floor. We set foot on the stairs leading up to the front porch and Lula stopped and sniffed. The smell of fried onions and burgers was being sucked out of the kitchen and hung in the air surrounding Zeta house. The cook was at work getting lunch ready.

"That smells good," Lula said, "but I got my mind set on crispy onion rings and that smells like plain old fried onions."

Splosh! Lula got water ballooned. Direct hit. I immediately jumped aside.

"What the Sam Hill?" Lula yelled. "Son of a peach basket." She looked at me. "What was that?"

"Water balloon, but it smells like it was filled with beer. I think it was a beer balloon."

Lula pulled her gun out of her purse, fired off a fast four rounds at the balcony, and everyone scattered.

"Good thing I remembered to bring my gun today," she said, squinting up at the balcony. "Did I hit anyone?"

"I don't think so."

"I had beer in my eyes."

Not that it mattered. Lula was a terrible shot. She had a six-inch lavender afro going today. She shook her head, beer sprayed out, and she looked like nothing had happened to her hair. She stripped off her orange tank top, wrung it out, and put it back on.

"Just like new," Lula said. "Lucky I don't mind the smell of beer."

We went inside and the room cleared.

"I want to talk to Brian Karwatt," I yelled. "Is Brian here?"

Silence.

"This don't seem like such a party house to me," Lula said. "All they got is one beer balloon. What's with that? Where'd everybody go?"

"I imagine they aren't used to being shot at."

"See, that's what's so good about living in my ethnic neighborhood. You get used to stuff like that. I live in a melting pot. We got illegal felons, legal felons, moron gangbangers, and some dopers. They're shooting at each other all the time."

"Maybe you should move."

"I suppose, but I can afford the rent, and I got a big closet. I figure I just have to sit tight and wait for it to get gentrified around me."

Lula lived in a small two-story Victorian-style house with gingerbread trim. The house was currently painted pink and yellow and lavender. It was the only house in the neighborhood with not a smidgeon of graffiti because if some idiot came near the house with a can of spray paint the lesbian owner would beat the crap out of him. The owner lived on the ground floor. Lula was one of two people who lived on the second floor. And a seventy-five-year-old woman lived in the attic. Apparently she thought she was Katharine Hepburn, but aside from that she managed very nicely, according to Lula.

We left the Zeta house and went to the student center. Julie Ruley wasn't in the newspaper office, wasn't in the food court, wasn't in sight.

"This beer smell coming out of my clothes is making me hungry," Lula said. "I need onion rings to go with the beer. I'm voting to move on to Billy Bacon."

Sounded like a good idea to me. We weren't getting anywhere with the Gobbles search, and I wasn't feeling a lot of love for Kiltman College. We heard a car alarm wailing when we got to the administration building. We rounded the corner and saw that the noise was coming from the Mercedes. I used my key fob to shut the alarm off, and Lula and I approached the car.

"There's a goose in your car," Lula said. She looked more closely. "There's a whole bunch of gooses. And they pooped on everything."

A small crowd had gathered on the fringe of the lot. Mintner was one of them.

"This has all the earmarks of a Zeta stunt," Mintner said.

"Somebody should let those gooses out," Lula said. "I don't think they're happy about being locked up in there."

Not happy was a vast understatement. The geese were in a blind rage, viciously pecking at the windows, shredding the leather seats, crapping their brains out.

The crowd took a step back. No one wanted to get in the way of the freaked-out geese.

"Maybe you should be the one to open the door," Mintner said to Lula.

"I don't see what the big deal is," Lula said. "They just want to get out and go about their business."

Lula opened the door, and the geese rushed out at her. There was a lot of wing flapping and Lula shrieking. It was like she was caught in a goose blizzard, and then they moved on, hurling themselves at whoever got in their way. Everyone but Lula and I fled to the safety of the building.

Lula stood dazed for a couple beats. The geese had pecked at her lavender afro and torn holes in her clothes. There were fresh globs of goose poop dotted across the pavement and a lot of honking in the distance.

"That's the gratitude I get for setting those stupid things free," Lula said. "Those geese are freakin' rude."

Ranger's black Porsche 911 cruised into the lot. Ranger got out, looked at the Mercedes, and smiled.

"*Do not smile*," I said to him. "This is all your fault for giving me a Mercedes. I was perfectly happy with my junky old car, but you had to come along and set me up for disaster. You *knew* this was going to happen.

85

You've probably been sitting around all morning, counting down the minutes until I destroyed the car. It's a record breaker, right? Headline: 'Stephanie Plum Destroys a Car in Less than Four Hours'."

Okay, so I knew I was out of control, but I couldn't seem to reel it in. I was doing a goose imitation, flapping my arms and yelling, pacing around.

"I am just *so aggravated*," I said. "Why me? Why do these things happen to me?"

"I don't know what you're complaining about," Lula said. "You didn't get no beer dumped on you. And you didn't get yourself pecked apart by a herd of pissed-off honkers."

Ranger slung an arm around me and hugged me into him, and I could feel him laughing.

"It's not funny," I said.

"Babe, I haven't got a lot of funny in my life. Let me enjoy the moment."

"You have a strange sense of humor."

"Most people think I have *no* sense of humor."

I pushed away and looked at him. "How did you happen along just now?"

"The control room picked up the break-in and reported it to me. I was in the area so I thought I'd come take a look. I got here just in time to see Lula open the car door." The smile returned. "I almost ran up on the curb when the geese flew out."

"I'm pretty sure someone at Zeta did this."

"Because you're looking for Globovic?" Ranger asked.

"Yeah. And Lula sort of shot up their balcony earlier today."

This didn't get a full-on smile from Ranger, but I saw the corners of his mouth curve the smallest amount, and I knew he was making an effort to control himself.

"We've got no way to get onion rings," Lula said. "There's wall-to-wall goose poop in our car, and they pecked up the steering wheel. I was counting on those onion rings."

"Hal is on his way. He'll take care of the Mercedes, and he'll take you back to the office," Ranger said to Lula.

"Hal is the one who looks like a stegosaurus, right?" Lula asked. "No neck. Lots of bulging back muscles? He's a good-lookin' guy. I wouldn't mind sharing some onion rings with him."

He also faints at the sight of blood and is terrified of Lula.

"I can ride with Hal, too," I said.

"I'd rather you came with me," Ranger said. "I want to talk to you."

We cruised out of the lot just as Hal was pulling in. I thought he went pale at the sight of the parking lot covered with goose poop, but it could just have been the lighting. Or maybe it was the sight of Lula waiting for him with her shredded clothes and goose-styled hair.

"I've already disposed of your previous car," Ranger said. "Would you like a replacement Mercedes?"

"No! I don't want to be responsible for the death of another Mercedes. Take me to my parents' house, and I'll borrow Big Blue until I find something else."

Big Blue is a '53 powder blue and white Buick Roadmaster. My Great-Uncle Sandor gave it to my grandmother when he went into the nursing home, and it's resided in my parents' garage ever since. Its only modern amenities are its jury-rigged seatbelts. Other than that, it drives like a refrigerator on wheels and sucks gas faster than I can pump it in. The good part is that it's free and indestructible.

"They did the autopsy on Doug Linken today, and they're releasing him to the family. There will be a viewing tomorrow night and the funeral on Thursday. Monica has asked for security for the viewing and funeral. Can I count on you for those days?"

"Yes. Just don't give me any more cars."

CHAPTER
TEN

My mother and Grandma Mazur were in the kitchen eating lunch when I walked in. Grandma Mazur came to live with my parents when Grandpa graduated from this life to the next. My mother, being a good Catholic woman, accepted this living arrangement as her cross to bear and gets by with help from Jim Beam. My father developed selective hearing and spends a lot of time at his lodge. And now that we took his gun away we feel it's safe to leave him alone with Grandma.

The house is a two-story, two-family duplex, which means it shares a wall with an almost identical house. It has a small foyer, a small living room crammed with overstuffed furniture and the television, a dining room that can seat ten uncomfortably, and a slightly dated but homey kitchen in the back of the house. There are three small bedrooms and a bathroom upstairs.

"You're in time for lunch," Grandma said. "We got ham and cheese sandwiches."

"That sounds good," I said, getting a plate and taking a seat at the small kitchen table.

My sister, Valerie, and I did our homework at the table when we were kids. She was the perfect one, and

I was less than perfect. She had a brief spell of blemished perfection when her first marriage went into the toilet, but she's since remarried and is now back on track for sainthood, producing grandchildren for my parents at an alarming rate.

"How's Valerie?" I asked. "I haven't talked to her in a couple days."

"She's big as a house, and she pees when she moves," Grandma said. "Hard to believe the baby isn't due for another month."

My mother made a sandwich for me. "Mustard or mayonnaise?"

"Mayonnaise."

"Your mother and I went to mass this morning and everyone was talking about Doug Linken," Grandma said. "About how someone knocked him off. Are you still babysitting his wife?"

"I'm signed on to provide security for the viewing and funeral."

"Boy, you've got the glamour job," Grandma said. "You probably get to go to the wake, too. I'd give my eyeteeth to go to that wake."

This wasn't much of a sacrifice since Grandma wore dentures. Not to mention she wasn't above crashing a wake.

"The girls at the bakery think it was the wife who whacked him. Everyone knew he fooled around. He went out to smoke, and good old Monica drilled a couple rounds into him," Grandma said.

"Terrible," my mother said. "Such a tragedy."

"I hear they're only having one viewing," Grandma said to me. "It's going to be packed. If you need extra muscle I'm available."

"If you involve your grandmother in this you'll be banned from having dessert at this house for life," my mother said.

"I won't need extra muscle," I said. "Ranger is the primary security. I'm only there if Monica has to go to the ladies' room."

"Will you be in a Rangeman uniform?" Grandma asked. "Will you be packing?"

"No and sort of."

"How can you sort of carry a gun?" Grandma asked.

"I don't have any bullets. I keep forgetting to buy them."

"I might be able to help you out," Grandma said.

My mother gave my grandmother the steely-eye. "Yesterday you told me you got rid of the gun and all the bullets. You *promised*."

"I was gonna suggest that she goes to Walmart," Grandma said. "They got everything."

I caught my mother glancing at the cupboard over the sink. She kept her hooch there, and she was probably weighing my opinion of her as an alcoholic against how bad she needed a drink. I love Grandma Mazur, but in all honesty, if I had to live with her I'd be taking a nip in the afternoon too.

"What kind of bad guys are you hunting down these days?" Grandma asked.

"No one special," I said. "The usual suspects."

"I heard you nabbed Billy Bacon but he got away," Grandma said.

I nodded. "We had him in custody but there was an incident."

My mother snapped to attention. "What incident? I didn't hear about an incident."

"It involved Lula," I said. "I was getting lunch for all of us and Lula and Billy Bacon got carjacked."

"Oh my God," my mother said, and immediately made the sign of the cross. "Where did this happen? It was in a bad neighborhood, wasn't it? You're always in a bad neighborhood. I don't know why you can't find a nice normal job."

"I sort of like my job," I said. "I have a lot of personal freedom, and I don't have to get dressed up."

"You make no money, and you're always dealing with criminals," my mother said. "It's a terrible job. You should quit and marry Joseph."

I blew out a sigh.

"What?" my mother said.

"I'm not ready to marry Morelli."

"Why not? He has a good job. He has a house. He has a nice car."

"He's hot," Grandma said. "Don't forget about him being hot."

I wondered if there was dessert. There was a white Tasty Pastry bakery box sitting on the counter.

Grandma saw me look over at it. "Italian cookies," she said. "Pinwheels and almond horns and pistachio shortbread." She got up and brought the box to the table.

92

"You're not getting any younger," my mother said to me. "What are you waiting for? You should bring him to dinner on Friday. I'll make pot roast."

I took a pinwheel. "We broke up."

My mother's eyes got wide. "Broke up? Why?"

I shrugged. "He dumped me."

"What did you do?" my mother asked. "You must have done something."

I made a show of looking at my watch. "Oh gosh, look at the time. I have to go. I was wondering if I could borrow Uncle Sandor's car."

"What happened to *your* car?" my mother asked.

"It's having some problems."

"Like what? Do you need new tires? A battery?"

"It got filled with geese," I said. "It wasn't my fault."

No point trying to hide it. It was probably going to be on the evening news. At the very least I was sure it would make YouTube. Everyone in the parking lot had had their cellphones out, recording the fiasco.

My mother looked dazed. As if someone had just smacked her in the face with a frying pan. "Geese," she murmured.

"It's okay," I said. "Lula let them out, and the geese were fine."

"Dang it. I miss all the good stuff," Grandma said.

I grabbed a couple more cookies, stood, and lifted my messenger bag onto my shoulder. "Gotta get back to work."

Grandma got the Buick's key out of the junk drawer and handed it to me. "I got bullets and an extra gun if you need it," she whispered. "Don't tell your mother."

★ ★ ★

I always felt like a failure when I drove Big Blue, because I only drove it when I had no other option. Big Blue represented rock bottom in the automotive department. Jay Leno would have thought it was ultra cool, but I just thought it was ultra hard to drive. And a '53 Buick wasn't in keeping with my self-image. Truth is, the Mercedes SUV wasn't compatible with my self-image, either. I was more a bright yellow Jeep Wrangler, or maybe a zippy red Hyundai.

I eased the blue behemoth out of the garage and onto the road. I put it in gear, fed it gas, and the car oozed forward. It picked up speed and rolled along like a tank. I turned out of the Burg onto Hamilton Avenue and noticed a red light flashing in my rearview mirror. It was Morelli in his green SUV with a *Kojak* light stuck onto his roof. I pulled into the small Tasty Pastry parking lot, and he pulled in after me. I got out of the Buick and held my hands up.

"Funny," he said. "Put your hands down before someone calls your mother and tells her you've been busted."

"What's up?"

"I saw you drive by, and I thought you would be interested in a ballistics report I just got back. The bullets extracted from Doug Linken and his partner, Harry Getz, are a match. They were fired from the same gun."

"So we've got one shooter. Do you have the gun?"

"No."

"Have you locked on to a motive?"

94

"The obvious is a disgruntled investor, but I'm having a hard time buying it."

"There are the wives."

"Do you think they're capable of murder?" Morelli asked.

"I wouldn't discount them, given the right circumstances."

"I agree, but I'm not sold on them, either."

"What *are* you sold on?"

"Nothing right now. The autopsy didn't tell me anything interesting. I'm waiting on some crime scene lab reports. I'm telling you this because it's my understanding that Ranger has been retained to provide security for the widow Linken. I'm assuming you'll be part of that party."

"You assume correct."

"I wouldn't mind if you snitched for me. I'll be attending both events, but I won't have the access you'll have."

"I thought you were handing over your gun and your badge."

"It's a process. There are things I have to set in place first."

"Another job?"

"Yeah. In the meantime I'm doing the one I have as best as I can."

"Gee, that's freakin' noble of you."

"Yep. That's me. Mr Noble."

"I don't get it. So you have heartburn. Big deal. Everyone has heartburn. That's not a good enough reason to stop being a cop. What are you going to do? Sell insurance? Manage a minimart?"

"Maybe."

"You never talked about this with me. We were practically living together, and you never said anything about this."

"It's something I have to figure out on my own."

I did an eye roll. "Men."

He leaned closer and I thought he was going to kiss me, but it turned out he was looking at my pimple.

"Is this it?" he asked.

"It's better than it was yesterday."

"And it's all my fault?"

"Yes!"

He rocked back on his heels and grinned. "Sorry about that."

"You don't look sorry."

"I am. I swear. Would you like a donut? Coffee?"

"No, but thanks. I need to go. Things to do."

I slid behind the wheel, and he looked in at me. "Nice seeing you," he said.

I did another eye roll. I couldn't help myself. I watched Morelli drive out of the lot, and then I backtracked a block from the bakery to the office and parked behind Lula's Firebird.

Connie looked up when I walked in. "Where's Lula?"

"She's with Hal. I think they're going to check out some onion rings."

"Rangeman Hal?"

"Yep. It's been *one of those days*. Zeta is trying to discourage us from looking for Gobbles. They bombed Lula with a beer balloon, and then they filled the Mercedes with geese."

"Real geese?" Connie asked.

"Yeah. It wasn't pretty. Anyway, long story short, Ranger dropped me off at my parents' house so I could get Big Blue, and Lula went with Hal."

"I ran all the fraternity brothers through the system and didn't get any hits around M and Hawthorne," Connie said.

The front door to the office burst open and Lula swung in.

"Holy bejeezus," Connie said, staring at Lula. "What happened to you?"

"Geese," Lula said. "Ungrateful sons-a-bitches."

"You have some goose feathers stuck in your hair," I told her.

"I know. I'm gonna have to go to the beauty salon and have Ayesha work her magic. I was thinking I needed a color change anyways. Lavender is pretty with my brown skin but it's limiting, you see what I'm saying? I might need to be a blonde on account of then I can move into the red section of my closet. I'm feeling in a red mood."

"Did you get Hal to take you for onion lings?" I asked.

"He didn't have time. We waited until the car got loaded onto the flatbed, and then he had to do a patrol run after he dropped me here. It's just as well since I'm thinking I'm going straight to Ayesha. And then after

I'm all beautified I might go out for the onion rings.
You all could go with me. It could be a girls' night out,
and we could even look for Gobbles. I've been thinking
about it, and I bet he comes out of his hidey-hole at
night."

"I'm in," Connie said. "I don't have anything going
on tonight."

"Sure," I said. "Me too."

"Almost forgot," Connie said to me. "You got
another package. Looks like it's from Daniel Craig
again. No return address. Handwriting looks the same."

Oh boy.

I opened the envelope and pulled out a photograph
of a totally ripped naked guy with a huge boner and
Daniel Craig's head. Clearly the head had been
photoshopped on.

"Daniel Craig got a good one," Lula said.

"It's not Daniel Craig," I said. "Someone put his
head on someone else's body. The skin tones don't
match."

"Too bad for Daniel Craig," Lula said. "He'd like to
own that bad boy."

Connie looked over my shoulder. "Is that a real
penis? It's massive."

"I've seen them come that big," Lula said. "Mostly
when they get that big they're kind of dumb. They
haven't got a lot of talent, if you know what I mean."

I didn't know what she meant, and I didn't want to
ask.

"There's something written on the back," Connie
said.

98

I turned the picture over and read the inscription. "It says *This is the real me*."

"I think *the real me* got delusions of grandeur," Lula said.

"Do you want the picture?" I asked Lula. "There's no bath caddy."

"I'll take it anyway," Lula said. "Things have been slow in the romance department."

CHAPTER
ELEVEN

I had a peanut butter and olive sandwich for dinner and by eight o'clock I was starving. I'd showered away the beer that had splashed off Lula's head onto mine. I'd put on clean jeans, a dressy tank top with a matching sweater, and flats, and I was ready for girls' night out.

I met Lula and Connie at the office fifteen minutes later. Lula had hair the color of daffodils. It was all braided into cornrows, and she had a bunch of extensions that reached her shoulders. She'd squashed herself into a fire-engine-red bandage dress that was intended for a much smaller woman but seemed to work for Lula. She had matching lipstick, and she was wearing matching fancy Louboutin knockoffs.

Connie was still wearing work clothes. Tight black pencil skirt that came to an inch above her knees, tight white scoop-necked top that showed a lot of cleavage, chunky gold necklace, earrings, and cuff bracelet, and gold wedge heels. Connie was a couple years older than me and a lot more Italian. My hair was out of control by birth. Hers was by design.

We all piled into the Firebird and Lula drove us to M Street and Hawthorne. We rode around several blocks before parking, keeping our eyes open for Gobbles.

"I'm going with the girlfriend," Connie said.

I had no opinion. I was thinking about Morelli. He was a really good cop. I couldn't imagine him being anything else. Of course, until a couple days ago I also couldn't have imagined him dumping me. Not that this was our first breakup. Morelli and I had a long history of breakups. None of the previous ones had been done naked. The naked thing was really irksome.

Lula parked, and we all sashayed into the bar and scoped it out. Two booths were filled. Four men were at the bar. No Gobbles.

We settled into a booth and ordered burgers and fries, onion rings, and a pitcher of beer.

"Do you ever think about getting a different job?" I asked Connie.

"Every day."

"Not me," Lula said. "I like my job."

"That's because you don't have one," Connie said. "You wander into the office when you feel like it. You drive Stephanie around. You make fried chicken and donut runs. And we pay you."

"That's true," Lula said. "It's real sweet. Best thing ever happened to me was when the office burned down, and we went from paper files to digital. I came in as a file clerk, but now there's hardly anything to file. Fortunately I'm of other value. I have intimate knowledge of the worst parts of town and the most disgusting people, and I annoy Vinnie."

We raised our beer glasses and made a toast to annoying Vinnie.

"You really get dressed up for a girls' night out," Connie said to Lula.

"You bet your ass. I take pride in my appearance." She looked down and made a boob adjustment, hoisting the girls up a couple inches. "You never know when Mr Good Enough is gonna come along. I like to be ready."

Connie looked across the table at me. "Why did you ask about changing jobs? Are you thinking about changing jobs?"

"I know someone who's making a big change, and it has me thinking."

"What would you do if you stopped working for Vinnie?" Connie asked.

The food arrived, and I ate an onion ring and thought about life after Vincent Plum Bail Bonds.

"I have no clue," I said to Connie.

"What did you want to be when you were a little girl?"

"Wonder Woman."

"I get that," Lula said. "She had that golden lasso. And her boots were excellent."

"I wanted to be Madonna," Connie said.

I finished my burger and went to talk to the bartender.

"I remember you," he said. "You and some guy who looked like Batman chased a guy who ran up a thirty-dollar bar tab through the kitchen and that was the last I saw of him."

"He's not a regular?"

"Not nearly."

"Did he say anything while he was here? Did he talk to you?"

"No. What are you, a cop?"

"Bond enforcement."

I gave him a twenty and returned to the booth.

"How'd that go?" Lula asked.

"Gobbles hasn't been back."

"He's in the Zeta cellar," Lula said. "I got a feeling. It's almost a vision except there's fog so it's not one of my more clear visions."

"So you think we should go look in the cellar?"

"Not we. I think you should look in the cellar," Lula said. "I just had my hair done, and I'm wearing my nice red dress. And we're not sure what they did with those geese. They could be in the cellar protecting Gobbles."

"Your vision doesn't tell you about the geese?"

"I don't see no geese, but that doesn't mean there aren't any of them there. Like I said, there's some fog in the vision."

"I guess it wouldn't hurt to take a look around the Zeta house."

Lula parked in a handicap space behind the student center and placed a handicap permit on her dashboard.

"This'll disguise my car so it doesn't get filled with geese," Lula said. "You'd have to be a real horrible person to put geese in a handicap car."

I examined the parking permit. "Where did you get this?"

"Macy's," Lula said. "Jimmy the Cheat was having a trunk sale in the parking lot."

"You bought a handicap parking permit from a man called Jimmy the Cheat? Weren't you afraid of getting cheated?"

"Hell no. I've known Jimmy forever. Anyways I looked it over real careful, and it looked like the real deal."

"You're not handicapped," Connie said.

"There's all kinds of handicaps," Lula said. "I had a disadvantaged childhood and I'm afraid of snakes. I even think I might have some dyslexia and gluten issues. I was putting this dress on, and I was thinking I might have some bloat."

I didn't want to hear bloat details, so I led everyone across the dark campus to the Zeta house. We stood in deep shadow for a while and watched people coming and going. Lights were on in the house, and music was blaring.

"Do you still think he's in the cellar?" I asked Lula.

"I don't know anymore," she said. "I was pretty sure at first, but there's this fog sort of blurring out my video."

"For crying out loud," Connie said. "Let's get this over with and look in the cellar."

"They keep the door locked," I told her.

"So we walk in, find someone of authority, and tell him to unlock the door."

"It might not be that simple," I said. "Last time we were here Lula shot up the balcony."

"Yeah, but I didn't hit anybody," Lula said. "And look at these people. They drink all day long and they're all potheads. They probably can't remember anything."

"Okay, we'll go in, but no shooting," I said to Lula. "None. Zero. Zip. Do not even *think* about taking your gun out of your purse."

"Sure. I got that," Lula said. "We'll go in nice and quiet and look around without nobody noticing us. We'll just blend in and sneak around to the cellar door. It might even be unlocked."

I thought our chances of going unnoticed were slim. I was with a two-hundred-pound black woman wearing a size two knock-your-eyes-out tube of red spandex that barely covered her ass. Her hair was blond. Her cleavage was comparable to the Grand Canyon. Her nipples were practically punching holes in the spandex fabric.

"Good plan," I said. "Let's go in and keep a low profile."

We made it through the entrance hall and living room and I stopped to look around.

A guy came up to us with plastic cups of beer. "Are you ladies students here?"

"Hell, yeah," Lula said, taking a cup. "We're studying all kinds of shit."

"Anyone want to go upstairs?"

"Mostly we want to go downstairs," Lula said.

"We'd like to see the cellar," Connie told him.

"The cellar's locked," he said. "Nothing going on down there anyway."

"Then why is it locked?" I asked.

"We keep the beer down there," he said.

"I want to see the beer," Lula said. "I get turned on by beer. Most people want to drink it, but I like looking at it. You can't imagine what I could do to you if I had enough beer to look at. You'd never be the same. You'd be ruined when I was done with you."

"Damn," he said. "I haven't got a key. Professor Pooka has a key. So what's it going to be? One or all of you want to make me happy?"

"You're gonna have to get happy all by yourself," Lula said. "We don't make people happy until we know them better. We got standards."

"How much do your standards cost?" he asked Lula. "What can I get for ten bucks?"

"You can't get nothin' for ten bucks," Lula said. "If I was in that business, which I'm not, I wouldn't even look at you for ten bucks."

"How about twenty? I bet I could get a tug from you for twenty."

"This here's insulting," Lula said. "Do you know what you could get for twenty? You could get a snootful of pepper spray. I got some in my purse."

Lula reached into her purse and pulled out her gun.

His eyes got wide and he jumped away. "Crap! I know who you are. You're the nut who shot up the balcony."

Someone yelled, "*She's got a gun! It's the shooter! Call the police, Run for your lives.*"

"I was just lookin' for my pepper spray," Lula said.

People were bolting up the stairs and out the front door.

"This isn't good," Lula said. "This here's pandemonium."

I turned Lula around and pointed her toward the kitchen. "Follow Connie!"

We ran through the deserted kitchen and out the back door. I smacked into Dean Mintner and knocked him flat.

Connie and I picked him up and set him on his feet.

"Sorry," I said. "I didn't see you here in the dark."

"What are you doing out here?" Lula asked him.

"I'm watching. I'm taking down names and collecting evidence."

"What kind of evidence?"

"I don't know yet," Mintner said. "I haven't figured it out."

"This is why I'm not going to college," Lula said. "Everybody's a goofball."

We left Mintner and hustled back to the Firebird. Lula put her handicap parking permit into the glove compartment and drove us to the office.

"This was a good girls' night out," Lula said. "We should do this more often."

CHAPTER
TWELVE

I woke up to the smell of coffee brewing. On the one hand terrific, and on the other hand terrifying, because it meant someone was in my kitchen. If it was a deranged killer he probably wouldn't be making coffee. That left Morelli with a key. And Ranger with the ability to magically unlock anything. My money was on Morelli. Ranger would have brought Starbucks coffee in a container. I got out of bed and padded barefoot into the kitchen.

Morelli was lounging against my counter with a coffee mug in his hand. He poured out a mug for me, added cream, and handed it over.

"I need to talk to you," he said.

"I have a phone. I have a *doorbell*."

"I tried your doorbell. It isn't working."

"You're lucky I didn't shoot you."

"Cupcake, your gun is in the cookie jar, and it isn't loaded."

I drank some coffee and pushed my hair off my face. "What do you want to talk about?"

"Doug Linken. We're starting to get toxicology tests back, and he had traces of black gunpowder on the soles of his shoes. Harry Getz had the same gunpowder on his shoes. It's not something you see every day. You might find it on a gunsmith or collector, but neither Linken or Getz owned a gun."

"Why are you telling this to me?"

"You're going to be with Monica Linken tonight. I've asked her about the gunpowder, but she had nothing. I thought you might be able to pick up something. Someone passing in front of the casket who might make his own ammo. Maybe a history buff who likes guns."

"Is Monica still a suspect?"

"She's a person of interest. She has a solid alibi on the Getz shooting. Getz's wife has a solid alibi on the Linken shooting."

"So now Getz and Linken were killed by the same gun, and they both had gunpowder on their shoes."

"Yep."

"Do they have anything else in common?"

"They were business partners."

"Maybe they were doing business with someone who used gunpowder."

"We've combed through all their transactions and can't find anything, but it's not off the table. Clearly they stepped in it somewhere."

"Why do you think it relates to the shootings?"

"I wouldn't go so far as to say it relates to the shootings. I just think it's an interesting piece of information. It's a mystery I wouldn't mind having solved."

I put a piece of bread in the toaster and looked at Morelli. "Do you want toast? Cereal?"

He shook his head no. "I've already eaten breakfast."

I had been sleeping in an oversized T-shirt and bikini panties. Morelli's eyes were focused on the hem of the T-shirt that hung two inches below my butt.

"Cute," Morelli said.

"Are you sure you came to talk about Doug Linken?"

He finished his coffee and rinsed his cup out in the sink. "Yeah. I'm really screwed up, right?"

"Looks like it to me, but what do I know."

He pulled me to him and kissed me. His hand slid under the T-shirt and moved to my breast, and his thumb teased across the nipple.

His phone buzzed with a message, and we both froze.

"Shit," Morelli said.

The message buzzed again. He removed his hand from my breast and checked the message.

"This is why I have acid reflux," he said. "Whenever I'm in the middle of *anything* someone gets murdered."

He gave me a quick kiss. He apologized and left.

This was the second time in less than forty-eight hours that a man stopped fondling me because his phone rang. And both times it was because someone had been killed. If I wasn't a well-adjusted, emotionally healthy person I might be bothered by this.

I spread peanut butter on my toast, sliced some banana onto it, and ate it while I drank my coffee and checked my email.

I deleted several offers for penis enlargement, and two offers from Russian women who wanted to meet

110

me. I answered an email from my friend Mary Lou, and I checked a couple news sites. I was depressed after the news sites so I played Pharrell Williams's video "Happy". I danced along with Pharrell into the kitchen, fed Rex and gave him fresh water, and I was ready to get on with my day.

An hour later I rolled into the office. Lula was on the couch with a copy of *Star* and Connie was at her desk. Vinnie's door was shut, but his car was parked in the small lot attached to the building.

"You've got a box," Connie said to me. "It was just delivered."

"It looks like the size of a shoe box," Lula said. "I bet it's shoes."

There was no return address and the postmark was out of state.

"I didn't order shoes," I said. "I didn't order anything."

I ripped the packing tape off, opened the box, and read the enclosed card.

"What's it say?" Lula asked.

"It says, *I found you! I'm smart like that. Here's something you can use until we meet in person. And it's signed Scooter Stud Muffin.*"

I pulled out a wad of tissue paper, and we all stared into the box.

"It's a dildo," Lula said. "It's a good size, too."

Vinnie came out of his lair and looked at the dildo. "Cripes," he said. "That thing's big enough to pork a cow."

Lula took it out of the box and held it up for a good look. "It says here on the tag that it's called *The Whopper* and it got studs for her lady's pleasure."

Lula pushed a button on the scrotum and the dildo lit up and vibrated.

"This here's a quality dildo," Lula said. "It got a good hum to it."

"Who's Stud Muffin?" Vinnie asked.

"Stephanie got some secret admirers," Lula said. "They send her stuff but there's no return address or name. Unless you count *Stud Muffin* as a name."

"That's real interesting," Vinnie said. "It would be even more interesting if you put the rubber wanger away and did some work. I'm not running a charity here. Why isn't Billy Bacon back behind bars?"

"We can't find him," Lula said. "He's slippery."

"So set a trap. Do *something*."

Vinnie went back into his office and slammed and locked his door.

"Setting a trap isn't a bad idea," I said. "We should give him a pizza party."

"I like it," Lula said. "A big man like him doesn't pass up food. Especially if it's free. We'll send them to his mama's house. I'm sure she knows how to get in touch with him."

"I have a cousin working at Domino's," Connie said. "I'll order it. How many do you want?"

"Has to be enough to tempt him," I said. "Send him four extra-large with the works. Have the delivery person say it's part of a promotion, and he was picked out at random. Tell your cousin we want it delivered at noon."

"Domino's is the best," Lula said. "They got everything there. They even got gluten free. Maybe you should include one that's gluten free in case Billy Bacon got issues."

"Do we know anyone who would have gunpowder?" I asked Connie.

"My Uncle Lou," Connie said. "He's old-school. Likes to make his own shells."

"He must be eighty," Lula said. "Is he still whacking people?"

"He gets the occasional job," Connie said. "He has easy access to nursing homes. Blends right in. Mostly these days he does mercy killings. Terminal cancer. Advanced Alzheimer's."

"Besides Lou?" I asked.

"I know some people making explosives," Lula said.

"Terrorists?" Connie asked.

"Gangbangers," Lula said. "Not all that dangerous since they all flunked out of school and can't read. Pretty much they blow the fingers off their hands putting the shit together wrong."

The door to Vinnie's inner office got yanked open again and Vinnie stuck his head out. "What are you doing still sitting there? You think the rat bastards we bail out are going to come to you?" He pulled his head back in and slammed the door shut.

"That man has a personality problem," Lula said.

"Yeah, that's the tip of the iceberg," Connie said. "He's also got father-in-law problems. We're not running in the black this month, and Harry isn't happy. Do you remember Ernest Blatzo?"

This got a grimace out of me. Blatzo was a high-money bond who went FTA and disappeared off the face of the earth.

"It would help a lot if you could find Blatzo," Connie said. "He's worth twice as much as Billy Bacon and Ken Globovic combined."

He was also a freak. He raped women in very brutal ways. It was suspected that some of the women he raped got chopped up into tiny pieces and fed to the pack of feral cats that lived in his yard. Since those women were never found it was hard to pin a murder charge on him. I wanted to see him behind bars, but I wasn't excited about coming face-to-face with him. Truth is, I wasn't all that brave. My successes were the result of stubbornness and dumb luck. Lula wasn't that brave either. She caught people by accidentally running over them with her car or promising them a night of hot sex and then sitting on them until I showed up.

"I have his file in my bag," I said to Connie. "I was hoping he was out of country."

"We have a source who tells us Blatzo is back in his old house. No one's actually seen him, but his herd of feral cats are back."

"I could throw up thinking about that," Lula said. "That's disgusting."

I headed out. "Later," I said to Connie. "Confirm the pizza party."

"I'm on it," Connie said. "What do you want me to do with the *thing?*"

114

"Toss it," I told her.

"That would be a shame," Lula said. "It's an expensive piece of equipment. I'll take it if nobody else wants it. I bet I could get good money for this on eBay."

Connie handed the dildo over to Lula, and Lula shoved it into her purse.

"Do you want the box?" Connie asked.

"Negative," Lula said. "It's easier this way."

We got to the curb and looked at the Buick and the Firebird.

"What's it going to be?" I asked Lula.

"I'm thinking Buick. Just in case we get lucky, I don't want to put Billy Bacon back in my Firebird."

"No problem."

We chugged away, and I took a left on Broad.

"I don't like the looks of this," Lula said. "You're going looking for Blatzo."

"We'll do a drive-by in his neighborhood. If we see any cats gnawing on body parts we'll call the police."

"I got creepy crawlies thinking about it. I'm gonna have nightmares tonight."

Blatzo lived in a hard-times, drug-infested neighborhood of dingy little cinder block houses squatting on blighted, neglected lots. Junker cars and rusted-out refrigerators were left to linger in the front yards. Rats served as target practice in the backyards. The best you could say about Blatzo's street was that it was free of the gangbangers who lived on Stark. Here the gangbangers only stopped by occasionally to visit the meth lab that flourished two doors down from Blatzo's.

I idled in front of Blatzo's house, and Lula and I looked up and down the street.

"Don't look like anybody's home," Lula said. "No lights on. No car in the driveway. Weeds don't look trampled. No cats sitting on the stoop. Are we sure Blatzo is still living here?"

"According to Connie. His name is on the lease as a renter, and someone is paying the rent."

"Are you gonna go look around?"

"I'm thinking about it."

"Well, you could think about how you're gonna do it all by yourself because I'm not walking out in that yard. There's snakes."

Lula had a point. Hard to tell what was living in the tall weeds and trash.

"There's a path to the house," I said. "I'm going to knock on the front door."

"Are you nuts? What are you gonna do after you knock? What if he answers?"

"If he answers I'll cuff him."

"The man is six foot tall, probably weighs as much as a Volkswagen, and eats raw meat."

I got out of the car and tucked cuffs into my right back pocket and pepper spray into the left.

"Do you have a gun?" Lula asked.

"I have a stun gun."

"Does it work?"

I took the stun gun out of my bag and turned it on. "Yep," I said. "It's charged."

116

"I got another one of those feelings," Lula said. "It's a premonition of disaster."

"Chances of Blatzo being in the house are minuscule," I said. "I'm going to knock on the door. No one will answer. Case closed."

"I like that thinking," Lula said. "That makes sense. I could even take a video with my cellphone to show Vinnie we did something."

I squared my shoulders, tipped my chin up, and marched across the street to the house. Lula got out of the Buick and started filming. I got halfway up the path to the front door, eyes on the prize, and I stepped on a snake. I shrieked and jumped. The snake slid away into the weeds. And I ran back to the car.

"Should I stop filming?" Lula asked.

"Yes. Get into the car."

I retraced my route to Broad and parked in front of the hardware store. I went into the store, bought high rubber boots, and drove back to Blatzo's house.

"I don't know if those boots are snake-proof," Lula said. "What if you come on a snake with big fangs? Or a jumping snake?"

I got out of the car and put the boots on. "This time I'll watch where I'm walking."

"Do you want me to film?"

"I don't care."

"You sound cranky," Lula said.

"I'm a little stressed."

"You'll feel better after the pizza party."

"The pizza party isn't for us."

"Yeah, but there might be some left over. Wouldn't want to waste good pizza."

I stomped off in my big boots. Across the street, up the path, onto the small stoop. I rang the bell, the door opened, a big hairy hand reached out, grabbed me by my shirt front, and dragged me into the house. The door slammed shut and I blinked up at Blatzo.

"Ernest?" I asked.

"Yeah."

"You n-n-need to come with me. You're in violation of your bond."

"I don't feel like doing that. You know what I feel like doing?"

Oh crap. He was going to rape me and chop me up into tiny pieces for his cats.

"I feel like having a party," he said. "Just you and me."

"Yeah, that would be good. We'll have a party after we check you in with the court."

"We'll have a party *now*."

He still had my shirt in his fist, and when he said *now* he jerked me off my feet and slammed me against the wall.

I yanked the stun gun out of my pocket, pressed the go button, and rammed the prongs against his neck.

His eyes lost focus for a split second but there was no further reaction.

"I don't like that," he said. "That's not a nice thing to do to a man who invites you to a party."

I kicked out at him, and he backhanded me across the face.

118

The front door opened, and Lula stuck her head in. "Everything going okay in here?"

"No!" I said. "Shoot him. Shoot him!"

Lula reached into her purse and pulled out the dildo. "What the hell?" Blatzo said.

Lula threw the dildo at him, it bounced off his forehead, and he bent to pick it up.

"Run!" I said to Lula.

We bolted out of the house and across the street, and jumped into the Buick. My hand was shaking so bad I couldn't turn the key in the ignition.

"He's coming! He's coming!" Lula yelled.

I got the engine to crank over, I slammed the gas pedal to the floor, and we motored off, leaving Blatzo standing in the middle of the road. I had a white-knuckle grip on the wheel, and my heart was skipping beats.

"I thought I was going to be cat food," I said to Lula. "I hit him with the stun gun and he barely blinked."

"I left my dildo there," Lula said.

"No kidding. What was the deal with the dildo anyway? I told you to shoot him, not make love to him."

"Mostly you don't make love to a man with a dildo," Lula said. "Maybe if you're another man. I don't know too much about that side of it."

"Why didn't you shoot him?"

"I meant to, but the dildo was on top, and I pulled it out by mistake. I guess it was just easy to wrap my hand around in a panic. You know how you go for something familiar."

I looked down and saw that my shirt had splotches of blood on it.

"You got a cut on the corner of your mouth," Lula said.

"I kicked him, and he smacked me."

"I told you I had a feeling. I had a premonition of disaster."

"It wouldn't have been such a disaster if you'd pulled your gun out of your purse instead of your dildo."

"This is the first time I've seen him up close. He's not an attractive man," Lula said. "And I think he'd been drinking."

CHAPTER
THIRTEEN

I drove out of Blatzo's neighborhood and stopped at the bonds office to clean up.

"Whoops," Connie said. "What happened to you?"

"I found Ernest Blatzo."

"And?"

"He hit me. Lula threw the dildo at him. We ran for our lives. Next time I'll take Ranger."

"I got video," Lula said to Connie. "You gotta see this. Stephanie stepped on a snake."

I went to the powder room and stared at myself in the mirror. My lip was puffy but not terrible. The cut wasn't serious. Painful, but not needing stitches. A bruise was forming on the right side of my face. I washed the blood away and put a Band-Aid over the cut. Not much I could do with the shirt.

"I called the pizza in," Connie said when I came out of the powder room. "Do you want me to cancel?"

I shook my head no. "I'm fine." I looked over at Lula. "Let's roll."

"Are you sure you're okay?" Lula asked. "You got a eye twitch."

"What land of a person has no reaction to a stun gun?" I asked.

"He might be on drugs," Lula said.

"You think?"

"Probably be best if I drive the Buick this time," Lula said. "You look like you got road rage coming on."

"I need a donut. I'll be fine if I just get a donut or four or five."

"Ordinarily I'd think that was a fine idea," Lula said, "but you might not want all that sugar what with the pimple and the eye twitch."

"*I want a donut and I want it now!*" I yelled at Lula.

I looked over at Connie. "I'm out of control, right?"

"Yeah," Connie said. "Pretty much. Maybe you want to dial it back."

"I've been under a lot of stress lately."

"You know what I do when I got stress?" Lula said. "I go shoe shopping."

"I knit," Connie said.

"Get out!" Lula said. "I never knew you knit stuff."

"I don't knit *stuff*," Connie said. "I just knit."

Vinnie stuck his head out of his office. "You know what I do?"

"We all know what you do," Lula said. "And we don't want to hear about it."

Vinnie pulled his head back into his office and slammed and locked the door.

"How about instead of a donut we bogart one of those pizzas," Lula said. "That'll fix you right up."

I followed Lula out of the office and buckled myself into the Buick. "I want a donut," I said. And a tear leaked out of my eye.

122

"Yeah, I could see that," Lula said. "Don't you worry, I'll get you some donuts. And then we'll wash them donuts down with pizza."

Holy cow, I was a mess. I stepped on a snake, got hit in the face, ruined my shirt, and lost a boyfriend. I could deal with it all but the boyfriend. It added up to too much. Morelli had sucker punched me. I hadn't seen it coming. I was trying to take it in stride, but truth is it was increasingly painful.

Lula drove to Tasty Pastry and parked at the curb.

"You go in and get whatever the hell you want," Lula said. "This here's emergency donuts."

I returned ten minutes later with two boxes. "I got two of everything," I said. "And four Boston Kremes. And I put in a job application."

"A what?"

"They're looking for a baker."

"You can't bake. You can't boil an egg."

"I could learn."

"Are they willing to teach you?"

"They didn't say. I thought I'd buy some books and watch the cooking channel."

"You got a good job. Why do you want to be a baker?"

I ate half a Boston Kreme. "I don't know. It just came over me. I used to work at Tasty Pastry when I was in high school. I was a counter girl."

Lula ate a maple glazed while she drove. "Did you ever work at baking?"

"No, but I watched *Ratatouille* about a dozen times."

"That was a cartoon about rats."

"It was inspiring."

Lula turned off Hamilton and headed north toward K Street.

"We need a plan for catching Billy Bacon," Lula said. "We're not gonna be able to bribe him with lunch when he's got all that pizza on his doorstep."

"I thought we'd walk in when he's eating, and you can distract him while I cuff him."

"I guess that's a okay plan. And if that don't work you can stun gun him, but you don't want to use pepper spray around the pizza."

I ate a second Boston Kreme.

"You feeling better?" Lula asked.

I nodded. "I just had a moment back there."

We parked across the street from Billy Bacon's apartment and waited for the pizza delivery. A little car with a Domino's sign on it pulled to the curb in front of Billy's building and a young guy got out with four pizza boxes. He looked over at us and gave us a thumbs-up.

He disappeared into the building and reappeared five minutes later.

Lula leaned out the driver's side window toward him. "How many people in the apartment?"

"One," he said. "An older woman in a nightgown."

He got into his Domino's car and drove off.

Twenty minutes later we still didn't see any sign of Billy Bacon.

"He should have showed up by now," I said to Lula. "I can't imagine him going out of the neighborhood.

This is the only entrance to the apartment building, right?"

"I never checked. I thought you checked."

Crap.

Lula and I left Big Blue and crossed the street to the building. We climbed the three flights of stairs and listened at Billy's apartment door.

"I can hear him," Lula whispered. "He's talking to his momma, and he's eating my pizza."

I knocked on the door and the talking stopped.

I knocked again and Eula told us to go away.

"You're gonna have to kick the door in," Lula said to me.

Kicking doors in is not a skill I've mastered. Ranger and Morelli are experts. Me, not at all.

"Not going to happen," I said to Lula.

"I could shoot the lock off," Lula said.

"No!"

"How about if we both run at it together and put our shoulder to it?"

I hammered on the door. "Open up. Bond enforcement."

The door got yanked open and Billy Bacon rushed out and knocked Lula and me over like we were bowling pins. He ran past us and thundered down the stairs with a pizza box under his arm. Lula and I scrambled to our feet and took off after him.

I chased him out of the building and caught up with him a half block away. I grabbed the back of his shirt and hung on, but I couldn't stop him.

"Incoming," Lula yelled. "Outta my way."

I released Billy Bacon, jumped to the side, and Lula threw herself at him, knocking him to the ground. He went down face-first with Lula on top of him. He was still holding the pizza box.

I snapped the cuffs on him, and Lula rolled off.

"I skinned my knee," Billy Bacon said, sitting up. "Look at what you did. You tore a hole in my pants."

"Is this here a whole pizza?" Lula asked him.

"Yeah. Ma and me didn't get to it."

Lula opened the box and looked inside. "I might need a piece."

"I won it in a contest," Billy said. "It was a major award."

We hoisted Billy Bacon up to his feet and trundled him across the street to the Buick. We buckled him into the backseat, gave him the rest of the donuts, and Lula and I each took a piece of pizza.

"You're going to get me out of jail again, aren't you?" Billy asked us.

"As soon as we can," I told him. "I'll call Connie and tell her you want to be bonded out."

"I can't eat these here donuts with my hands behind my back," Billy said.

I took a donut out of the box and crammed it into his mouth.

It was almost two o'clock when Lula and I got back to the office. I gave Connie the body receipt certifying that Billy Bacon Brown was in police custody, and Lula gave Connie the last two pieces of pizza.

"Are we going to spring Billy Bacon?" Lula asked.

"If the court sets bail," Connie said. "And if he can come up with something as security. Vinnie was already downtown, so he said he'd look in on him."

"He's not such a bad person," Lula said. "He's just not smart."

"Gotta go," I said. "Things to do."

"Like what?" Lula asked.

"Things," I told her. "Email, laundry, thinking."

"I'd help you out with all that," Lula said, "but I gotta finish reading my *Star* magazine. I gotta see what's happening with the Bieber."

I left the office and chugged off in my Buick. I parked in my apartment building lot, took the stairs to the second floor, and stopped in front of my door. There was an FTD flower arrangement sitting there. I carted the flowers inside and read the card.

Happy Birthday. Sorry I couldn't be here to celebrate it with you. Kenny.

First, it wasn't my birthday. Second, I didn't know anyone named Kenny who would be sending me flowers. Third, it was definitely my address on the card. Four, no return address for Kenny.

I could see getting weird mail at the office. I gave out business cards to all sorts of people. At one point Vinnie had my picture on a billboard. And there was the occasional newspaper story about me burning down a mortuary or creating chaos at a bingo game. It bothered me that someone sent flowers to my apartment, though, because I was careful about giving out my home address. Although, now that I thought about it, my apartment had been fire-bombed a couple times, so clearly it wasn't impossible to find me. At least it was flowers this time and not a dildo.

I left the flowers on the kitchen counter and said hello to Rex. He was in his soup can and didn't acknowledge me. Probably he'd had a tough night running on his wheel and was still exhausted. I knew how he felt. I didn't have a lot of gas left in my tank, either.

I went to my computer and googled pastry schools. I'd fibbed to Lula about the email and laundry. I'd really wanted to come home and look into baking. I mean, how hard can it be? You follow a recipe, right? Chances of stepping on a snake and getting hit in the face were small in a bakery. The pay couldn't possibly be any worse than what I'm making now. And I would wear a cool white pastry chef coat.

I searched around and found there were a couple programs at local junior colleges, and a bunch of online courses. Or I could go the do-it-yourself route and download some cake recipes. Sort of do a test-drive to see if I liked *baking* cakes as much as I liked *eating* cakes.

I found a recipe for chocolate layer cake that looked straightforward. I'd never made a cake on my own, but I'd watched my mom and Grandma Mazur make tons of cakes. I printed out the recipe and made a list of ingredients, including two cake pans.

I had plenty of time until Ranger was due to pick me up so I trekked out to the supermarket and got everything I needed to make a cake, plus a six-pack of beer, a bag of chips, and lunch meat for sandwiches.

"This is exciting," I said to Rex, when I got back to my kitchen and lined my ingredients up on the counter. "This could be my dream job. This could be my life's work. It's possible that I was always meant to be a pastry chef and just never realized it before now."

Rex was nosing through the litter on the bottom of his cage, looking for hidden food treasures. I dropped a single Frito corn chip into his cage and he was beside himself with happiness. This is why hamsters are better than boyfriends. It doesn't take a lot to make a hamster happy.

CHAPTER
FOURTEEN

I was waiting outside when Ranger drove up. I was wearing a black skirt, a stretchy red top, a white linen jacket, and black flats. The bruise on my cheek was green, black, and blue. I went with extra mascara to balance out the cheek color, and I substituted first-aid ointment for lip gloss.

"Babe," Ranger said when I slipped into the Porsche.

It was more question than greeting.

"Ernest Blatzo didn't feel like going back to jail," I said.

"And?"

"And so, he didn't go."

"Would you like help?"

"Yes."

"We'll do it tomorrow morning," Ranger said. "I don't want to walk through his snake-infested yard at night."

No kidding.

We parked in the lot and waited at the side entrance of the funeral home for Monica to arrive.

"Do you think she's in any danger?" I asked Ranger.

"Without a motive for the two killings, it's hard to say who's in danger."

The front doors hadn't yet opened for mourners, but the parking lot was nearly full, and a large crowd was gathered on the porch, spilling down the stairs and onto the sidewalk in front of the building.

A black Rangeman SUV stopped in front of us and Monica Linken got out. The short skirt on her skin-tight fuchsia dress rode up high on her thigh, and her boobs almost jiggled out of the low scoop neck. She tugged her skirt down and leaned toward Ranger and me.

"I'm not wearing any underwear," she said.

"You're in good company," I told her. "Neither is Ranger."

This got a smile out of Ranger.

We took our places at the head of the casket, and Monica hauled out her electronic cigarette and powered up. The funeral home director asked her if she'd like a few moments alone with her husband, and Monica said she'd already had too many, thank you.

The double doors to Slumber Room No. 1 opened, and people poured in. Grandma Mazur was at the front of the crush. She half ran the length of the room and was third in line to see the deceased. She would have been second but Myra Campbell elbowed her out of the way at the last minute.

"So sorry for your loss," Grandma said to Monica. "My condolences."

"Yeah, whatever," Monica said.

Grandma leaned into the casket for a close look.

"What are you gonna do, kiss him?" Monica asked.

"I was trying to see where they cut him up when they took his brain out," Grandma said.

Monica sucked in some fake smoke. "You'd have to unzip his pants for that one."

Forty-five minutes later Monica was fidgeting and looking around.

"I need a drink," Monica said.

"Water, coffee, tea?" I asked her.

"Vodka straight up. How long is this creep show going to last?"

"The viewings usually go to nine or ten o'clock," I said.

"They don't expect me to stay the whole time, do they?"

"It's customary."

"I don't even know any of these people. Like that scary old lady in the first row. Who the hell is she?"

"That's my grandmother."

"Oh yeah, now I remember."

Grandma looked at me and winked and patted her purse.

At 8:15 p.m. Monica announced that she was leaving. "Tell the undertaker guy to keep this thing going as long as he wants," Monica said. "I'm going to slip out. It's not like I'm essential here. This is Doug's party, right?"

Morelli was standing at the back of the room a couple feet from the door. Our eyes met and I shrugged. The shrug said I had nothing. I hadn't been able to talk to Monica.

I saw him take out his cellphone, and a moment later a text message buzzed on my phone.

How did you get the bruise and cut lip? Morelli texted.

Ernest Blatzo, I texted back. *I'm fine.*

Even from this distance I could see a muscle clench in Morelli's jaw. I expected it went hand in hand with acid reflux.

"Where are you going?" I asked Monica.

"I'm gonna find a bar that's got lots of vodka."

"I could go with you."

"Really?"

"Sure. I like vodka. And you might need security."

Not to mention I needed to snitch for Morelli.

"Babe," Ranger said to me. "You working for a bonus?"

"I live to serve."

"I'll remind you of that when we drop her off and I take you home."

Whoa. I got a rush that went from the pit of my stomach straight to my doodah. Best to ignore it, I told myself. Serving Ranger would come to no good. He was an amazing lover and friend but his journey was ultimately solitary. He had things in his past that were shaping his future. I didn't know what they were but I knew they couldn't be ignored.

We called the funeral director over and explained that Monica needed to leave.

"Is she sick?" he asked.

"Yes," we said. "The emotional strain was just too much."

He nodded. "This happens," he said. "Unfortunately the deceased has no one else here. Who will greet the remaining people waiting to pay their condolences? Who will give last comfort to the deceased?"

"Grandma," I said.

The funeral director looked alarmed. "Grandma? Surely you don't mean Edna Mazur?"

"Yep," I said. "Edna was very close to the family."

"Oh dear," he said. "She's a nice lady, but I don't think —"

I waved Grandma over to the casket.

"What's up?" Grandma said.

"The widow needs to leave, and we thought since you were so close to the deceased you might be able to fill in."

"Stand at the head of the casket?"

"Yes."

"Hot damn. I'll do a real good job." She looked into the casket. "What was this guy's name again?"

"Doug."

"Don't worry about a thing. Me and Doug are going to get along just fine."

The funeral director bit into his lower lip, made the sign of the cross, and stepped back a couple paces.

Monica, Ranger, and I quietly slipped out the side door, and the Rangeman SUV pulled up.

"I don't want to go in this," Monica said. "I want the hot sports car."

Ranger handed me the keys to his 911 Turbo. "Have fun."

134

We buckled into the Porsche, and I turned the engine over.

"Anyplace special?" I asked her.

"Lotus."

Lotus was known for being a big hook-up spot. I'd never been inside, but now that I didn't have a boyfriend it seemed like something to investigate. The alternative was to allow my mother to fix me up with the butcher. I would prefer not to have this happen.

Lotus was on a side street in the center of the city. I took Hamilton to Broad and turned off Broad onto Merchant. I pulled into the small lot attached to Lotus and saw the Rangeman SUV cruise down Merchant and make a U-turn. Ranger was in protective mode.

"So tell me about your late husband's friends," I said to Monica. "I'm curious. Are you suspicious of any of them? Did he hang out with any gun enthusiasts?"

Monica freshened up her blood-red lipstick without benefit of mirror. This was something I'd never been able to accomplish.

"His friends were all boring. Nobody was interesting enough to have a gun. They talked about real estate and stocks and bonds, and rehashed college. Harry and Doug were fraternity brothers at Kiltman. They belonged to Zeta. Maybe Doug's girlfriends had guns. I didn't know any of his girlfriends."

"He had girlfriends?"

"Yeah, thank God. Otherwise *I* would have had to fuck him. He thought I didn't know he was bringing women into the house when I was away. Hell, if I'd had their address I'd have sent them all fruit baskets."

135

Cripes, this was disturbing. These people were all horrible.

"How about businesses he might have visited? Anything gun-related?" I asked her.

Monica got out of the Porsche and tugged her dress down. When she tugged it down her boobs popped out.

"Honestly," she said, pushing her boobs back into the dress. "Do I look like someone who would give a flying leap about his business?"

"Yes. The business brought money into the house."

"There were no gun-related businesses that I knew about. What's with the questioning?"

"Just curious."

"Yeah, right. I almost believe that. Are we going to stand out here all night, or what? I need a drink."

She wasn't the only one who needed a drink. This day wasn't going down as my all-time best. And on top of everything else that went wrong, I'd just flunked interrogation.

"Let's do it," I said. "Lead the way."

The exterior of Lotus was typical of the many bars in Trenton and almost identical to the two other bars on Merchant Street. Redbrick exterior, oak door, small neon sign over the door spelling out "Lotus", blacked-out windows. The interior looked like a bordello. Red walls, red upholstered banquettes, high-gloss black bar running the length of the room, high-gloss black trim on the banquettes, a bunch of high-top tables and chairs, fake candles on the tables. Flat-screens behind the bar tuned to sports stations. Lighting was dim to nonexistent. The

136

banquettes and high tops were all in use. People were standing two deep at the bar.

"Hey, you," Monica yelled at one of the bartenders. "My husband just died and I need a vodka."

I held my fingers up indicating we needed *two* vodkas.

Two seats opened up after ten minutes and Monica elbowed her way in. We ordered sliders from the bar menu and two more vodkas.

"This is supposed to be the big hook-up place," Monica said to me. "All I see are old losers. It's like they bused these people in from Happy Meadows Rest Home. My asshole husband looks better than most of these men and my husband is *dead*."

I had to admit I was surprised at the age of the crowd. Never having participated in the hook-up scene I'd always imagined a little more glamour.

"Can we have a serious discussion for just a moment?" I asked Monica. "Do you have reason to believe your life is in danger?"

"You mean other than my husband and his partner getting murdered?"

"Just because they were murdered doesn't necessarily mean you're a target."

"Yeah, but how do I know?"

She had a point.

"I can't even disappear," Monica said. "I'm a person of interest. I have to stay in town. How crap-ass is that?"

She wolfed down two sliders and ordered another round of vodkas. I was still working on my second vodka.

"Cripes," she said, looking at my vodka glass. "I'm drinking with a freaking amateur. Man up, for crying out loud."

"I'm not that good at drinking," I said.

Monica knocked back the third vodka. "Practice, practice, practice."

Monica slid off her barstool a little after eleven o'clock. "I'm done," she said. "Take me home."

I'd managed to choke down three drinks and my world was out of focus. I was hoping Ranger was waiting in the lot because otherwise it was going to be an Uber night.

Monica and I marched arm in arm out of the bar and my wish came true. Ranger appeared at my side, and a Rangeman SUV drove up. Monica was trundled into the SUV, the door was closed, and the car disappeared into the night.

"I'm trashed," I said to Ranger. "Take me home and put me to bed."

"Babe."

CHAPTER
FIFTEEN

I woke up in Ranger's bed. Ranger was no longer in it, but it was clear that he had been. This is what happens when you tell a man to put you to bed and you don't specify *which* bed. I felt around and determined I was wearing panties and one of Ranger's T-shirts. I suspected I'd had help with the undressing. And I vaguely recalled Ranger tucking me in. The fact that I was still wearing panties was a good sign. I'd hate to think I had an event with Ranger and couldn't remember it. That would be a horrible waste of guilt.

The room was cool and dark. A sliver of light peeked from behind a curtain. My iPhone had been placed on the bedside table. It was almost eight o'clock. I had a text message from Morelli telling me to call him.

Ranger owns a nine-story office building on a quiet, mostly residential street in downtown Trenton. He has underground parking, state-of-the-art security in the entire building, and a private apartment that occupies the top floor. The apartment is professionally decorated and feels right for Ranger. Clean classic lines, warm browns, and black leather. It's slick and comfortable but feels impersonal. There are no family photos displayed, no trinkets brought back from vacations, no clutter. The apartment is kept pristine by his housekeeper, Ella. His T-shirts are neatly folded. His dress shirts and slacks are perfectly ironed and hung. His guns are kept in locked drawers. Everything is easy to arrange because he only wears black.

His bathroom is Zen and ultra modern. His bedroom is luxuriously calm and unpretentiously masculine. His towels are fluffy. His sheets are smooth. The scent of Bulgari Green shower gel lingers on everything he touches. I'd marry him if for no other reason than to inherit Ella and his expensive linens.

My clothes had been draped over a chair in the dressing room. A note was pinned to the clothes. It told me to help myself to breakfast and to take the car in parking space number twelve. He reminded me that the Linken funeral was at eleven, and I had to be at the mortuary chapel at ten-thirty. Crap!

I got dressed, grabbed a bagel from the kitchen, and took the elevator to the basement garage. A shiny black Porsche Macan was in parking space number twelve. The key was on the dash. I jumped in and took off. By nine o'clock I was in my apartment, in my shower. No time for a hangover. I had my hair dry and pulled into a ponytail by nine-thirty. I washed a couple Advil down with a mug of coffee, brushed my teeth, and grimaced at myself in the mirror. The bruise was even worse than it had been yesterday.

I ransacked my closet, looking for something appropriate for a funeral, preferably something without gravy or bloodstains. I settled on an ancient black suit with a pencil skirt, and I dressed it up with heels. I grabbed my bag, yelled goodbye to Rex, and took off at a run. I called Morelli from the car.

"Did you have any luck last night?" Morelli asked.

"I didn't pick anything up at the viewing, but as you know I didn't stay for the whole thing. Monica wanted to leave so I went with her."

"I'm told you went to Lotus."

"Monica needed a drink and a hook-up."

"And?"

"She got lots of drinks," I told him. "There was slim pickings in the hook-up department."

"Yeah, there's an older crowd at Lotus these days thanks to Viagra. Used to be we had to worry about guys bootlegging roofies. Now it's little blue stiffie pills. Gives all the swingers from the seventies a second chance to get an STD. Were you able to get anything from Monica?"

"Nothing useful. She's halfway afraid she's on the hit list, but she's hostile about getting questioned. And I think her brain is too pickled to hold a thought."

"Thanks for trying. I appreciate it. I'll see you at the funeral."

"Don't get too close to me. I'm making a huge effort to be civil, but deep down inside I'd really like to punch you in the face."

"Understood."

Ranger was in the funeral home lot waiting for me when I skidded to a stop and parked. He was in a perfectly tailored black suit, black dress shirt, and tie.

The Glock at his waist was undetectable and didn't ruin the line of the jacket.

I got out of the Macan and made an attempt to smooth some of the wrinkles out of my skirt. "Thanks for rescuing me last night," I said. "And thanks for the car loaner."

"It's part of my fleet, and it's a permanent loaner. At least for as long as it lasts. You can't go around collecting felons in a '53 Buick. You're too recognizable."

People were beginning to gather for the funeral, pulling into the lot and lining up on the street.

"This is going to be a circus," I said to Ranger. "Is the widow here yet?"

"She's with the deceased, having a last moment alone with him. I have Tank babysitting her."

"You're going to have to give him a bonus for this one."

"He's getting the weekend off," Ranger said.

We went inside and inserted earbuds with battery packs so we could communicate. The plan was for me to sit with Monica and for Ranger to stand at the back of the chapel. When the service was over Ranger and I would ride in the funeral home limo with Monica. Tank and Hal would follow in an SUV. The entire rest of Trenton would follow Tank and Hal.

Monica was wearing a skin-tight black sheath dress, her usual spike heels, and very dark oversized sunglasses.

"How do I look?" she asked me. "Do you think the television SAT truck will cover this?"

142

"I didn't see the truck out there," I said, "but it's early."

The service was short. No one tried to shoot anybody. No SAT truck showed up. Afterward we whisked Monica out the side door and into the limo. She took a flask out of her purse and chugged something that smelled like turpentine.

"When this is over I'm checking myself into Betty Ford," Monica said. "Then after my liver enzymes go down I might allow myself a small drinkypoo once in a while."

Good luck to Betty Ford.

It started raining halfway to the cemetery.

"Are you fucking kidding me?" Monica said. "Rain? Could this day get any worse?"

A small canopy had been set over enough folding chairs for the immediate family. The rest of Trenton huddled under big black mortuary umbrellas. A chair next to Monica had been reserved for me, and I saw Grandma knock a couple people aside to secure a chair. I looked out over the rest of the mourners and recognized a few people from the Burg. Professor Pooka was there and also Dean Mintner.

"Do you know Professor Pooka from the Kiltman biology department?" I asked Monica.

"He's a fruitcake. He came to Doug with a research project that needed funding. He came knocking on our door one night. Totally uninvited. Looked like a maniac. Practically foaming at the mouth about some crazy discovery."

"Why did he come to Doug?"

"Doug was on a bunch of committees at Kiltman. He liked being a big-shot alum doing fundraising and shit."

"Did Doug help him get the funding?"

"No. No one would fund Pooka and he was turned down for tenure. That's all I know. Doug didn't go into detail with me. He saved the chatter for the sluts."

Spending time with Monica wasn't doing a lot to enhance my opinion of marriage. Actually, it wasn't doing much to enhance my opinion of human beings in general.

The priest was saying something about Doug Linken, but it was hard to hear him over the rain falling on the tarp. He made the sign of the cross and looked to Monica. The funeral director gave Monica a red rose, and Monica threw it at the casket.

"Done," Monica said, standing. "Let's eat. I ordered vodka rigatoni from Marsilio's for the wake."

The wake was held at the firehouse in the room usually reserved for Tuesday bingo. There was a full serve-yourself bar, two tables of donated food in disposable containers, and enough vodka rig to feed two hundred people. I stayed close to Monica, Ranger watched from twenty paces, and Morelli hung in a corner and never took his eyes off me. He was in jeans, a blue buttoned-down shirt, a red and blue striped tie, and a navy blazer. It was the middle of the day, but he had a five o'clock shadow that looked good on him. The hem on his jeans had wicked up water. Aside from the jeans he seemed untouched by the rain.

144

I wasn't doing as well as Morelli. My hair had frizzed up into a giant afro-type ponytail. My suit was damp and my shoes squished water.

"This is a real bust," Grandma said, sidling up to me. "I like when the wake is in a house and you get to see people's furniture and the kind of toilet paper they buy. This was hardly worth crashing."

"Did you get anything to eat?"

"I had some vodka rig and Mabel Worchek's meatball casserole. I'm thinking about going back for a piece of cake. There are some good-looking cakes there."

"I've been thinking I might bake a cake."

"Get out."

"I found a recipe, and I bought a couple cake pans."

"What brought this on?"

"It just came over me," I said.

"You aren't pregnant, are you?"

"No!"

"Well, just holler if you need help. And people are asking about that bruise you've got. It's a pip. What am I supposed to tell people?"

"Tell them I got it in a bar fight."

"Can I say you got hit by a drag queen?"

"Sure."

"It would make a more interesting story," Grandma said.

Monica was standing behind me and I heard her give a snort of laughter. "I'd take a day off from work to see you get punched out by anyone."

"I thought you didn't have a job," I said to Monica.

"Yeah, but if I did."

I looked around the room for possible suspects. In the movies the criminal always returns to the scene of the crime, always shows up at the funeral. Most of the people who showed up for this wake were same old same old. Professional wake attendees. The couple people I recognized from Kiltman had only been present at graveside. Obviously the politically correct gesture didn't extend to the wake. Obviously they didn't know about the vodka rig.

"I'm soggy," Monica said. "I want to go home. Grab one of those trays of vodka rig and meet me outside."

"Copy," Ranger said into my earbud.

I found a tray that was mostly untouched, covered it with aluminum foil, turned to leave, and bumped into Morelli.

"You could get into big trouble taking that vodka rig," Morelli said. "That's official wake property."

"I'll chance it."

He gently traced his fingertip across my bruise. "I hate to see this."

"You realize you're risking that punch in the face."

"Yeah. Go ahead, take your best shot. I deserve it."

"You're only saying that because I have my hands filled with casserole."

"True. Are you planning on having this for dinner?"

"Monica asked me to grab it for her."

"Anything strike you as odd today?" Morelli asked.

"Other than the fact that the widow is showing no remorse?"

"You'd think she could at least pretend, right?"

"I think she's in a transitional place," I said. "Moving on with her life."

"That's charitable."

"And she drinks a lot."

"That's real. I was looking for more than that. There was a weird-looking guy at graveside. He wasn't part of the usual funeral crowd."

"The guy wearing pajamas?"

"Yes."

"That's Stanley Pooka. He's a biology professor at Kiltman. Doug Linken was a Kiltman alum. Active in fundraising and stuff. Dean Mintner was also at graveside."

Ranger's voice came into my earbud. "Kiss him goodbye and get out here with the food."

"Gotta go," I said to Morelli.

Monica was waiting in the SUV when I brought the vodka rig to her.

"Do you need further security?" Ranger asked her.

"No, but I wouldn't mind keeping the two gorillas in the front seat for a couple hours of fun."

"Their shift ends at four," Ranger said.

"It won't take that long," Monica told him.

They drove away and Ranger wrapped an arm around me. "We missed our date with Ernie Blatzo this morning. Do you want to take him down now or wait until tomorrow?"

"Tomorrow. Definitely tomorrow."

"You need to get out of your wet clothes, Babe. I'd be happy to help."

"Thanks for the offer, but you've helped enough."

CHAPTER
SIXTEEN

I kicked my shoes off when I walked into my apartment, and I left my wet clothes on the bathroom floor. I took a fast shower to wash the smell of funeral flowers out of my hair, and I dressed in sweats and a T-shirt. It was the moment of truth. I was going to bake a cake.

Rex was running on his wheel when I walked into the kitchen.

"I'm going to bake a cake," I told him. "It's going to be awesome."

Rex stopped running for a moment, blinked his shiny black eyes at me, and went back to running. Not impressed.

I'd never seriously looked at my kitchen before, but it turns out I haven't got a lot of counter space. I also haven't got a mixer or a big bowl. I had a mixer when I first moved in but it got charred when my apartment was fire-bombed.

"No problem," I said to Rex. "I'll make my cake at my parents' house."

I packed my cake pans and all the cake ingredients into a shopping bag, laced up my sneakers, hung my messenger bag on my shoulder, and told Rex he was in charge of the apartment. The rain had slowed to a drizzle, and it looked like the sun was trying to burn through. I parked in my parents' driveway just as Mrs Kulicki was dropping Grandma off from the wake.

"Too bad you couldn't stay longer," Grandma said to me. "Emily Root had too many highballs and started singing one of them Miley Cyrus songs and tried to hump the fire pole. She was doing pretty good, too, considering she's so old."

"I don't think I know Emily Root."

"She was wearing the purple dress. They bused her in from Senior Living. She had her teeth in her purse on account of they were giving her trouble." Grandma looked at my shopping bag. "What have you got in there?"

"My cake stuff. I thought I'd make it here."

"Good idea. There's nothing better than smelling a cake baking in the house."

Grandma went upstairs to get out of her wet clothes, and I went into the kitchen.

"I came over to bake a cake," I told my mother.

My mother stopped chopping vegetables and made the sign of the cross. "Something's wrong. You have breast cancer. You found a lump."

"No!"

"You're pregnant."

"I'm fine. I just feel like making a cake."

"Holy mother! Where did you get that bruise?"

"I walked into something."

I unpacked my bag and set everything on the kitchen table. "I was going to make the cake at home but it turns out I don't have a mixer. Or a bowl. So I brought everything here."

"Maybe you should start with a box mix. I've got Duncan Hines in the pantry."

"Nope. I'm making it from scratch. If this turns out I might go to school to be a pastry chef."

My mother clapped her hand to her heart. "You got fired. The bonds office burned down again. Somebody finally killed Vinnie."

"Everything is fine. I just got to thinking it might be fun to bake cakes."

"There's got to be a reason for this. Did Joseph propose? Did he give you a ring? Would you like to learn how to roast a chicken?"

"No, no, and no. Joe and I broke up, remember?"

Grandma came into the kitchen. "What did I miss?"

"Stephanie and Joseph are still on the outs," my mother said.

I pulled the recipe out of my bag and put it on the counter. "I'm going to make a chocolate cake. And I'm going to make it all by myself."

"Good for you," Grandma said. "Go for it."

"All I have to do is follow the recipe, right?"

"Right," Grandma said. "And then we can eat it for dinner. We're having pasta and red sauce and meatballs, if you want to stay. We got a lot of it."

"Sure. That sounds good."

"I don't know why you keep breaking up with Joseph," my mother said. "He's such a nice young man."

150

This was true. But he didn't want me. It was so painful I couldn't say it out loud.

"I have to concentrate on this cake," I said. "I don't want to mess up."

"Last time you tried to cook something you set your kitchen on fire," Grandma said.

"Baking is better," I said. "It doesn't involve oil that suddenly bursts into flames."

I measured everything out and precisely followed the directions. I looked at the two cake pans.

"It says I'm supposed to dust them with flour," I said to Grandma.

"Yeah, but first you got to grease them up," Grandma said.

When I was done I had chocolate cake batter and flour all over the front of my T-shirt.

"Guess this is why pastry chefs wear those white jackets," I said.

"I always wanted one of them jackets," Grandma said. "We should get ourselves a couple. I could get them online."

"No more Internet," my mother said to my grandmother. "You're addicted. You're on all the time."

"I've got my sites," Grandma said. "I gotta keep up. I'm famous. I've got a blog."

I slid my cake pans into the oven and set the timer. "What kind of sites do you go on?"

"All the usual. I tweet and I google and I got a Facebook page. And I go on some dating sites, only they're the kind you don't date in person. You just date online. Some of those I stopped using because the men got weird."

Thwack! My mother sliced a carrot.

Grandma rolled her eyes. "She don't approve of me having fun," Grandma said.

Thwack! Another chunk off the carrot.

A text message buzzed on my phone. It was Lula wondering where I was hiding. I told her I was at my parents' house, and she texted back that she'd be there in a couple minutes.

"What kind of frosting are you putting on your cake?" Grandma asked.

"Chocolate."

"That's the best kind," Grandma said. "You wash out your bowl, and I'll set the butter on the counter to soften."

I just finished cleaning my work area when Lula showed up.

"Howdy, Mrs P. and Granny," Lula said. "Hope you don't mind me stopping by like this, but I had to bring a package to Stephanie. Connie said it could wait until tomorrow, but I gotta know what's in it."

It was a large padded envelope with no return address. It was postmarked Des Moines.

Oh boy.

"I bet it's something good," Lula said. "The excellent mechanical device we got came from Des Moines."

"Maybe we should wait until after dinner," I said.

"No way," Grandma said. "I want to see what you got."

I opened the envelope and pulled out a pair of skimpy black lace panties.

"They look like they got something missing from them," Grandma said.

"They're made that way," Lula said. "They're crotchless. I bet he got these at Frederick's of Hollywood." Lula looked in the bag and found a note. "It says here that he wants to rip these off Stephanie with his teeth."

My mother took a bottle of whiskey from the cupboard above the sink and poured herself two fingers, straight up.

"Why me?" my mother asked, tossing the whiskey back like a pro.

"There's a name on this card," Lula said. "It's the same as last time. Scooter Stud Muffin."

"That's a coincidence," Grandma said. "I used to friend someone who called himself Scooter Stud Muffin. I haven't heard from him in a while on account of I blocked him from my account. He was one of the ones that was getting weird."

"You mean like Facebook friend?" Lula asked.

"Yeah, only it wasn't Facebook," Grandma said. "It was a romance site."

Lula shook her finger at Grandma. "Granny, you've been catfishing!"

I looked over at Lula. "What's catfishing?"

"It's when you go on a dating website and make up your profile," Lula said. "Like Granny could be telling men she's twenty-three years old and a NFL cheerleader. Problem is when it gets serious and they want to meet you in person you gotta keep making excuses."

"Exactly," Grandma said. "I'm real hot stuff online."

"That's awful," my mother said.

"Everybody does it," Grandma said. "It's not like there's a lot of good stuff to watch on television these days. You got to do something to make the time go. You heard about fantasy football? This here's fantasy dating."

"Wait a minute," I said. "Let's see if I can guess. You told these men you were me?"

"Of course not," Grandma said. "You don't steal someone's identity. I went by the name of Gina Bigelow. And I said I was an interior designer. The only thing I borrowed from you was a picture. It didn't have your name on it or nothing."

"They could do an image search," Lula said. "Connie uses stuff like that at the office all the time. You just plug Stephanie's picture in, and it'll get you her name. After you have her name it's easy to find out all kinds of other things, like where she works and her home address."

"I didn't know that," Grandma said. "Does it work for everyone?"

"Some people are harder to find than others," I said. "I'm easy because my picture's been in the paper a couple times."

"And it's easy to find people who got social media accounts with their pictures on them," Lula said.

"It's like we're living in a time of magic," Grandma said.

"How many people are you catfishing?" Lula asked Grandma.

"I got two on the hook right now. And there were four that I cut loose. Those were the ones I sent the picture to. It was like a goodbye gesture."

"Boy, you must be something to get these men so worked up over you," Lula said. "I bet you would have made a good 'ho."

"Coming from you that's a real compliment," Grandma said to Lula.

"I smell cake baking," Lula said.

"It's Stephanie's cake," Grandma said. "She made it all by herself. We're going to put the frosting on it when it's cool."

"I wouldn't mind having a piece of that cake," Lula said.

"You could stay for dinner," Grandma said. "We're having the cake for dessert."

Lula looked over at my mother. "Is that okay with you, Mrs P.? I don't want to impose."

My mother is a good Christian woman who would never refuse someone a seat at her table, but I knew this was a nightmare for her. With Lula and Grandma at the table together, it's much more likely that my father will try to stab someone with his fork.

My father has developed coping methods over the years. He puts his head down at the dinner table and plows through the meal, listening to no one. Once in a while he'll pick his head up and look like he wants to join the Foreign Legion. At the moment he was concentrating on shoveling in chocolate cake.

"That was a wonderful meal," Lula said to my mother. "And this chocolate cake is excellent. Who'd ever think Stephanie could make a cake?"

"How about you?" Grandma asked Lula. "Do you like to bake?"

"I've never thought about baking," Lula said. "I think I'm more a savory person than a baking person. Not that I'd ever pass up a donut. And, anyways, I don't have a oven."

I finished my cake and wondered if *I* was a baking person. The cake had turned out okay. It had tasted better than it looked. It had been a little lopsided, and I couldn't figure out how to get a nice swirly pattern in the frosting.

Truth is, the whole thing hadn't been as satisfying as I'd hoped, and I couldn't imagine being in the back room of a bakery making cakes all day. I clearly was no Julia Child. And for sure I was no Martha Stewart.

I helped my mother clear the table and I paused in the kitchen to check my email. Two emails from Valerie with pictures of her kids. An email from Connie saying a new FTA had come in. And an email from Gobbles saying he wanted to talk to me. I emailed back asking when and where, and he answered that he wanted to meet me behind the Zeta house at ten o'clock. Good deal!

I pulled Lula aside and told her about the email.

"I'm in," Lula said. "We're gonna bust him."

"Don't you find it strange that he wants to talk?"

"He's probably just tired of being on the run."

"He could go to the police station and turn himself in. He doesn't need me."

"Maybe he doesn't know that."

"He's not stupid. And he has his girlfriend helping him. And she's not stupid."

"So what are you saying?"

"It feels complicated."

"Say what?"

I handed Lula a towel and we started drying the dishes my mom was washing.

"I just don't want to go all animal on him," I said. "I want to give him a chance to talk."

"I get that," Lula said. "I'm all about that."

"No shooting."

"Sure. Unless it's necessary."

"I don't think it's going to be necessary."

"Yeah, but if it is."

"*It won't be.*"

"Boy, you know how to take the fun out of stuff. What are we gonna do until ten o'clock? I wouldn't mind going to the mall. Macy's is having a shoe sale."

"I can't go to the mall like this. I've got chocolate cake batter all over my shirt."

"It balances out the bruise and the pimple," Lula said. "You don't know what to look at first. It's one of them things that confuses the senses. It could be a signature look for you."

"How about if you go to the mall without me, and pick me up at nine o'clock."

CHAPTER
SEVENTEEN

Lula and I parked in the student center lot at nine-thirty and walked across campus to the Zeta house. It was a dark moonless night. It was midweek and you might think Kiltman students would all be studying. Wrong. Half of Kiltman was at the Zeta house. Lights were blazing and a band was playing. We walked onto the porch and looked in at the band. Keyboard, two guitars, and a drummer.

"They aren't bad," Lula said, "but that drummer isn't no Brian Dunne."

"Do you see anyone in there who looks like Christopher Robin?"

"No. It's too packed to see anything."

We left the porch and walked around the side of the house. Gobbles said he'd meet me in the back. It was pitch-black at the back of the house. No exterior lighting and not a lot of light spilling out windows. They had a bunch of bushes that hadn't been maintained.

"I need a flashlight," Lula said. "I can't freakin' see where I'm going."

It didn't help that she was wearing platform FMPs.

"I think you're heading into the bushes," I said. "Go right."

"How far right? Where are you? Oh shit!"

There was the sound of Lula crashing into a bush, a grunt, and silence.

I flicked the flashlight app on my cellphone and aimed it at Lula. "Are you okay?"

"Yeah. I tripped over something. God knows what these loser college kids leave laying around."

I played the light from the phone around Lula. She was sprawled on the ground, and it was clear that she'd tripped over a body. The body was on its back, had an arm in a sling, and a hole in its head. It was Mintner, and I was pretty sure he was dead. His eyes were open but fixed, and he'd leaked a lot of blood. A bolt of cold fear and revulsion ripped through me, and I swallowed back a rush of nausea.

"M-M-Mintner," I said.

"Say what?"

"You tripped over Dean Mintner. I think he's dead."

I had my light trained on the body, but my hand was shaking, and the light was dancing around.

Lula scrambled away and jumped to her feet. "Holy shit. Holy crap. Damnation. I hate dead people. I'm gonna have the creeps. I touched him. I'm gonna have the death cooties. I need a shower. I need a cheeseburger. Someone get me fries."

I shut the flashlight app off and called Morelli.

"I'm at the Zeta house," I said. "Lula and I were walking around the house, looking for Gobbles, and Lula tripped over Dean Mintner. I'm pretty sure he's dead. Okay, I'm positive he's dead. He's got a bullet hole in his head."

I hung up with Morelli and flashed the light around the area. I didn't see any more bodies, dead or otherwise.

"He's on his way," I said to Lula. "And he's sending a uniform. Give me your gun, and I'll stay here. You go out to the road and wait for the uniform."

Lula handed her gun over. "You know how to use this, right?"

"Sort of."

If I was going to keep working for Vinnie, I was going to have to learn some skills. Some self-defense moves. And I needed to be more comfortable with a variety of firearms. I needed to at least be able to confiscate a gun and make sure I didn't shoot myself in the process.

I was taking a lot of deep breaths, trying to calm myself. I had the flashlight app off, and I was standing in total darkness. I was listening for a footfall, but my heart was beating so loud in my ears, I wasn't sure I could hear an elephant approaching. My fear was that I was in the shooter's sights. That some nutcase serial killer freak was in the shadows, thinking maybe he should kill me, too. I'd moved away from the body, but I didn't want to leave and chance that the crime scene would be disturbed. Or that the body would disappear.

I saw police strobes flash in the sky, and moments later I heard Lula talking, and I saw the glare of the Maglite the cop was carrying. I put the gun on the ground and stepped away.

I knew the cop. Eddie Gazarra. I went to high school with him, and now he was married to my cousin Shirley the Whiner.

"Lula's gun is on the ground," I said. "You don't want to mistake it for the murder weapon. Maybe you want to let her put it back in her purse."

Eddie flicked a beam of light on the gun. "Is it legal?"

"Is your momma?" Lula asked him.

"I never saw that gun," Eddie said, moving the light over to the body.

Thirty minutes later the area was secure. It had been roped off with crime scene tape and lights had been set up. The band had packed up and gone home. The students attending the party were detained in the Zeta house. They'd be questioned one by one and released. The side yard was filled with EMTs, cops, a forensic photographer, the coroner, the first of the crime scene techs, and Morelli. Lula said she had the heebie-jeebies, so I sent her home.

"It looks like he hasn't been dead long," Morelli said to me. "So far we haven't found anyone who heard gunshots. The band was playing. No one was in this back area. Except you."

"Globovic asked me to meet him here at ten o'clock. He said he wanted to talk."

"Was he here?"

"If he was, I didn't see him. We were walking toward the back of the building, in the dark, and Lula tripped over Mintner."

Morelli popped a couple pills into his mouth.

161

"Breath mints?" I asked him.

"Stomach issues."

"Sorry."

"It's all your fault," he said.

"Jeez."

He grinned and hugged me into him. "I was kidding. It's not all your fault. It's only partly your fault."

"Boy, that makes me feel a lot better. I don't have any more to contribute here. Will anyone mind if I get Gazarra to take me home?"

"No one will mind."

I sat in the front with Gazarra so no one would call my mother and tell her I'd been arrested.

"What's with Morelli?" I asked Gazarra. "Is something wrong at work?"

"This is Trenton. Work is never good."

"Then why do you stay?"

"I want my pension."

"That's years away."

"Yeah, but it's something to look forward to."

"Why has Morelli stayed?"

"He's the job. He believes in it. He's good at it."

"He seems to be taking more antacids than usual."

"I noticed. I don't know what the deal is with that."

"He hasn't said anything to you?"

"Morelli's never been a big talker, but he's more distant than usual these days. And he's been taking time off. I figured if anyone knew what was going on, it would be you."

"He broke up with me."

"Wow. I didn't know."

Gazarra idled at the back door of my building. "Are you freaked out by the shooting?" he asked. "Do you want me to see you inside?"

"Thanks, but it's not necessary. I'm used to being freaked out."

"One of the many perks of law enforcement."

I waved him away and went inside. I took the stairs to the second floor and found Julie Ruley hunched in front of my door, waiting for me. I had a moment of panic. My instinct was to turn and bolt down the stairs, but my feet weren't moving.

"Where's Gobbles?" I asked Julie.

"He didn't come with me. He doesn't know I'm here. We were walking across campus to meet you, and we saw the police. At first we thought they were there for us, but then we heard kids talking about how there was a shooting. We watched for a while from a distance and then we took off. I heard someone say it was Dean Mintner."

"He was shot and killed."

"That's horrible. I didn't like him, but it's still horrible."

"You realize that you and Gobbles are suspects?"

"We had nothing to do with it. Gobbles had nothing to do with what happened to Dean Mintner the first time."

"Mintner thought there was something evil going on at the fraternity."

"There's nothing evil going on at the fraternity, but there have been some strange things happening. Gobbles and I thought we could poke around and figure it out, but we can't. We're not getting anywhere. We need professional help, and we're afraid to go to the police. They'll put Gobbles in jail."

"What makes you think *I* won't put Gobbles in jail?"

Julie shrugged. "You seem nice. Gobbles said we have to trust someone, and we picked you."

Oh great.

"What have you got so far?" I asked her. "You must have some idea what's going on. What are the strange things that have been happening?"

"You have to talk to Gobbles about it."

"Is he staying with you?"

"No. He won't tell me where he's staying. He said if I don't *know* anything then I don't have to *lie* about anything. I was hoping we could set up another meeting."

"Sure, but I need to bring someone with me. I'm not walking into a meeting with Gobbles alone."

"I'll tell him."

I also wasn't inviting Julie Ruley into my apartment. I watched her walk to the elevator, and then I let myself in and locked the door. I'd had a creepy, disturbing night, and I wasn't feeling brave or especially trusting.

I went to my kitchen, tapped on Rex's cage to say hello, and I burst into tears. I checked the calendar on the wall to see if that time of the month was coming up. Not nearly. Damn. I was a mess and I couldn't even blame it on hormones. I made myself a peanut butter and banana sandwich and washed it down with a bottle of beer.

"Okay, this is better," I said to Rex. "Maybe I was just hungry. And, anyway, a man was killed and someone should cry over that, right?"

I got my Smith & Wesson out of the cookie jar and set it out on the counter so I'd remember to buy bullets. I checked the door one more time to make sure it was locked. I went through my apartment and made sure there were no killers in the closets or under the bed. I had a second beer and I got into my jammies and crawled into bed with the lights still on. I woke up at three o'clock, and shut the lights off.

CHAPTER
EIGHTEEN

I was dressed and in the kitchen when Ranger called.

"Are you up?" he asked.

"I'm up and making coffee."

The lock tumbled and Ranger walked in. He didn't have a key. Didn't need one. He could pick a lock faster than it took me to insert a key. I was just happy he'd called before breaking in so he didn't scare the crap out of me.

He was wearing the standard Rangeman uniform of black fatigues. If you didn't look closely at the logo on the shirt and ball cap you might think he was part of a SWAT unit.

"I heard you had an interesting night," Ranger said.

"There's something bad going on at Kiltman. Mintner was on a rant to shut down the Zeta house, and he was shot and left for dead in their overgrown azalea bushes."

"What's the gun doing on the counter? It's usually in the cookie jar."

"I put it there so I'd remember to buy bullets."

"Babe," Ranger said.

I think he was amused.

I poured my coffee into a to-go mug, grabbed a frozen waffle, and rammed my feet into my big rubber boots. "I'm ready."

"What about the gun?"

"Um, no bullets."

"Take it."

I dropped the gun into my messenger bag and followed Ranger to the parking lot. He was driving a black Ford Explorer that I knew was a Rangeman fleet car. He took Hamilton to Broad and stopped at the hardware store.

My first thought was that he was getting boots like mine, but it turned out the hardware store sold ammo. Who would have thought? He waited while I loaded my gun. He gave his head a slight shake when I dropped one of the rounds onto the floor, but didn't say anything. He marched me out of the store and back into the car.

Conversation was minimal for the rest of the ride. Ranger was in the zone. He drove into Blatzo's neighborhood and parked one house down. We got out and Ranger strapped on a gun belt and shrugged into a Kevlar vest. He gave me a vest and a similar gun belt.

I looked down at the big black Glock that was secured to my thigh with Velcro straps. "I feel like Annie Oakley."

"The Glock is just for looks. Don't try to use it. You have a place on the belt for your S&W. Use the gun you're most comfortable with."

I shoved the S&W into the gun belt and grimaced. I wasn't comfortable with *any* gun.

Ranger stood hands on hips and looked at me. "I'm completely enamored with you, and I have no idea why."

"I'm cute?"

"Babe, there has to be more, but honestly I don't know what it is."

"One of life's great mysteries," I said.

He pulled me hard against him and kissed me. Our tongues touched and I got a first-class rush.

"I hope that's your gun I feel pressing into my stomach," I said.

"My gun is on the side of my leg."

"Oh boy."

"You're feeling my flashlight."

"Sure," I said. "I knew that. That was my second guess."

He stepped away. "Watch for the snakes when we go to the door."

"I'm prepared."

He looked down at my boots. "Are those your snake boots?"

"I bought them special for this."

He grinned at me. "And I thought you didn't know what you were doing. How did this go down last time?"

"I knocked on the door. He opened it. And before I could say anything he grabbed me and pulled me into the house."

"Any weapons?"

"I saw a shotgun by the door."

"Okay, let's try this routine again."

I followed a couple paces behind Ranger and moved to the side when he rapped on the door. No one answered. Ranger rapped again and I called out, "Bond enforcement."

Blatzo opened the door, saw me standing there, and started to reach for me when he spotted Ranger. He stepped back and went for the shotgun. Ranger grabbed him by the front of his shirt, lifted him off his feet, and threw him across the room. Blatzo hit the wall with a *wump!* that knocked the air out of him. He slid to the floor, and Ranger walked over and cuffed him.

"That was easy," I said to Ranger.

"Keep your eye on him. I want to walk through the house." Ranger came back moments later and called dispatch at Trenton PD for police backup. "We have a cache of weapons and suspicious items in the freezer," he told her. "We'll stay on the scene until someone gets here."

"Suspicious items?" I asked him.

"You don't want to know more. And you definitely don't want to look for yourself."

It took ten minutes for a squad car to reach us. A second one immediately followed. The four men got out and cautiously walked to the front porch, obviously aware of the snakes.

"Why are there so many snakes in this neighborhood?" I asked Ranger.

"The meth dealers and crazies bring them in and set them loose. It's cheaper and more effective than a guard dog."

I showed the first cop my paperwork for Blatzo. It gave me permission to enter and capture.

"Looks legal," he said. "How do you want to go forward? Do you want to take him in or would you rather we take him?"

"We'll let you take him, and we'll follow," Ranger said.

One of the cops walked into the kitchen and looked in the freezer. "*Whoa!*" he said. "Hey, Stan, come take a look at this."

Stan grimaced and looked at Ranger. "Am I going to wish I hadn't eaten that burrito for breakfast?"

"It might not have been a good choice," Ranger said.

I felt like the house was getting crowded, and it didn't smell all that great, so I tiptoed down the sidewalk, removed my gun belt, and waited in the SUV. An unmarked car cruised down the street and angle-parked in front of the house. A third squad car rolled in. Stan was on the front stoop. He was holding a roll of crime scene tape, looking like he didn't know what to do with it. No one wanted to venture into the high grass around the house.

Ranger and two uniforms appeared in the doorway with Blatzo. Blatzo was frog-marched to a squad car, shackled, and tucked into the backseat.

Ranger walked back to me and got behind the wheel. "This was a good bust," he said. "There's enough evidence in that house to put Blatzo away forever."

I gave an involuntary shiver. If it hadn't been for Lula and the dildo, it might have been *my* body parts that were found in the freezer.

170

It was noon when I swung into the bonds office, and Connie and Lula were working their way through a bucket of extra crispy fried chicken.

"We got this chicken to celebrate that you snagged Blatzo," Lula said. "There's a piece left for you."

I took my crispy chicken part and gave Connie the body receipt. "I'm sure you heard about Dean Mintner."

"Everyone heard," Connie said. "It was on morning television. National."

"I told Connie how I found him, too," Lula said.

"You didn't find him," I said. "You fell over him."

"Yeah, but I've been thinking about it, and I'm pretty sure I was guided there by my extra sensoring ability."

Connie looked past the chicken bucket on her desk to the large plate glass window that fronted the bonds office. "What does your extra sensoring ability tell you about the guy who's staring in the window at us?"

We all looked out at him.

"Maybe he's hungry, and he sees this empty chicken bucket only he doesn't know it's empty," Lula said. "He could have a hungry expression on his face."

He moved from the window to the door and stepped inside. "Stephanie Plum, aka Gina Bigelow?"

"Oh crap," I said.

"I recognize you from your picture. I hope you don't mind me showing up like this, but I had to see you. We had this great relationship and then you broke it off. I wonder if we could talk in private."

"Private isn't necessary," I said. "You have the wrong person. We never had a relationship."

171

"Where are you from?" Lula asked him.

"Des Moines."

"I knew it," Lula said. "He's Mr Dildo and Skanky Panties."

"I'm guessing these are your friends," he said, "so obviously they know about your problem with the head lice and toenail fungus. It's not a big issue for me. We can find a good doctor. One who won't molest you when he examines you. I'm sure, that had to be traumatic . . . even if it did cure your, you know, frigid problem."

"You gotta love Granny," Lula said. "She should be writing books."

"I'm confused," he said. "Who's Granny?"

"She's the woman taking your panties for a test-drive," Lula said. "You've been catfished."

A red scald started at his collar and rose up his face. "Seriously? You mean, like, lied to?"

He was about five foot five inches tall, in his forties, and balding. He had a spray tan that reminded me of Gulden's mustard, and I suspected his own shoes hid toenail fungus. He looked like he might be an okay guy if you didn't set your expectations too high.

"Think of it as a fantasy adventure," I said.

"Everything you wrote to me was so sincere," he said.

"I didn't write to you," I told him. "Someone borrowed my picture."

"Yeah, it was her granny," Lula said. "Maybe you want to meet her granny. She's more fun than Stephanie here anyways."

172

"How old is she?" he asked Lula.

"Real old," Lula said, "but she's got some kick left in her. You could get a couple good dates out of her."

His attention shifted back to me. "I'd rather date you."

"No," I said. "Not going to happen."

"We put your dildo to good use, though," Lula said. "We hit a serial killer in the head with it. Stephanie might be cat food right now if it wasn't for that big-ass dildo."

"Sorry you came all the way from Des Moines," I said.

"It's okay. This was a side trip. I'm at a dental convention in Atlantic City."

"Are you a dentist?" Lula asked.

"I sell floss. We have three new flavors this season. I'm expecting a lot of excitement over it."

Lula, Connie, and I didn't exactly know where to go with that announcement so we wished him good luck and told him to stay in touch.

"You never know with people," Lula said when he left. "Who would guess he'd have such stellar taste in dildos?"

"*Stellar*," Connie said. "Where'd that word come from?"

"It's my word of the day," Lula said. "I'm always self-improving. I pick a word out and use it all day and then it's mine. Today's word is *stellar*."

"When did you start doing that?" Connie asked her.

"Today," Lula said. "This is the beginning of a new Lula. So what are you doing now?" Lula asked me. "You going home to bake another cake?"

I took the new FTA file from Connie. "One cake was enough." I read through the file. "Jesus Sanchez. Wanted for theft of a lawnmower. Are you kidding me? If I catch him I'll make fifty dollars. And I'm not going to catch him because by now he's cutting grass in Guatemala."

"I just hand them over," Connie said. "I don't necessarily tell you what to do with them."

"I tell you what to do with them," Vinnie yelled from inside his office. "Go find that asshole. Fifty bucks to you is five hundred smackers to me."

I stuffed the file into my messenger bag. Maybe I could go to beauty school. I could be a hairdresser. It would be like making a cake only with hair. Creative, right?

"I have stuff to do this afternoon," I said to Lula, "but I might be on the prowl for Gobbles tonight. Can I call you?"

"Yep. You can count on me."

I went home and googled beauty schools. There were two in Trenton and one in Bordentown. One of the Trenton schools I could attend part-time. That would be perfect. I went into the bathroom and looked at my hair. Shoulder length. Brown. Curly. Now that the rain had stopped it was calming down. When I was in high school I'd ironed it to get it straight.

I heard someone knocking on my door. I went to the door and looked out the security peephole. It was Morelli. He was holding a package.

"And?" I said, opening the door.

"I ran into the UPS guy in the lobby, and I said I'd take this up to you."

"The UPS guy knows you?"

"He's my cousin."

"And you were coming here anyway?"

"Yeah. I'm on my way home, and I thought I'd stop by and tell you about the forensic report so far on Mintner."

"That's nice of you, but not typical. You don't usually share information about ongoing investigations with me. Even when I want the information. Even when I *beg* you for the information."

"Don't push it, okay? I'm trying to be helpful."

I raised an eyebrow. Not buying it.

"I needed an excuse to see you," Morelli said.

"Why do you need an excuse?"

"I dumped you, remember? You haven't punched me in the face yet. I'm giving you another shot at it."

"The moment has passed."

"Open the package. It says it's from someone named Kenny. Is this a new boyfriend?"

"Are you jealous?"

He took a beat. His answer was soft. Almost whispered. "Yes."

Okay, I was feeling much better now. I was torturing Morelli. I opened the package and took out a golden two-pound box of Godiva chocolates. The card said *Sweets to my sweetie. Kenny.*

"I can't compete with this," Morelli said. "I can't afford two pounds of Godiva."

I blew out a sigh. I couldn't do it. "It's not mine," I said. "Grandma's been catfishing with my picture, and I'm getting all these stupid presents."

That got a full-on smile from Morelli. "Your grandmother is awesome. Are you going to give this box to her?"

"No. I'm going to eat them."

I picked one out and popped it into my mouth, but Morelli declined.

"Watching my weight," he said.

"You look the same as always."

Truth is, he was perfect.

"Do you want to know about Mintner?" he asked.

I put the cover back on the box. "Yes. Tell me about Mintner."

"He was shot with the same gun that killed Getz and Linken. And he had black gunpowder on the soles of his shoes."

"Do you have a connection?"

"Kiltman. Two alums and a dean. Beyond that, no."

"Suspect?"

"No one who feels just right."

"Globovic?"

"Why?" Morelli asked. "Smart kid. Maybe too smart. A little bored. Uses up excess energy planning toga parties and pranks."

"He's accused of assault."

"I've read the arrest report, and I'm not convinced. Something happened that night and Mintner ended up with a broken arm. The break wasn't consistent with someone getting hit with a bat."

"Gobbles said Mintner tripped over an ottoman."

Morelli took a beat, his expression changed, and he went into cop mode. "Do you talk to Gobbles a lot?"

"Not a lot."

"That was an impressive bust you made this morning."

"I didn't have much to do with it. Ranger went in and did his thing."

"They tell me Stanley Stoley checked out the freezer and lost his breakfast burrito."

"I didn't look. Ranger did the walk-through. Are you sure you don't want a chocolate?"

"Positive. I have to go. Bob is at home, waiting to go for a walk."

Morelli left. I closed and locked the door, and had four more pieces of candy. I went back to the bathroom and looked at my hair again. Who was I kidding? I wouldn't make it as a hairdresser. I had no patience with hair. I didn't even like fussing with my own hair. I'd make a better auto mechanic than hairdresser.

I put the lid on the candy and retied the red ribbon. I'd run it over to Grandma when I got the chance. A text message buzzed my phone at five o'clock. Gobbles wanted to meet with me at ten in the Windward Dorm parking lot. I texted back that I would be there with Lula.

CHAPTER
NINETEEN

I ran the candy over to Grandma at five-thirty. This was a shameless ploy to mooch dinner.

"Look who's here," Grandma said, always happy to see me. "And just in time. We're having meat-loaf for dinner and your mother made enough for an army."

"Meatloaf sounds great," I told her. "Who's Kenny?"

"He's one of my catfishing people that I cut loose. He was a real sweetie pie. I hated to let him go, but he was talking about getting married, and I was afraid he was underage."

"You mean a minor?"

"No. I mean too young to keep up with. I'm pretty good, but there's a lot of maintenance you got to do with a younger man. I cut them off at fifty. You might want to take a look at Kenny. He's local and he has a good job. He's a payroll clerk at the button factory."

I had the flowers under one arm and the candy under another. "He sent you these. They came to my apartment, of course."

"Flowers and candy! Isn't he the one. And Godiva! That's a quality gift."

"He seemed to think it was our birthday."

"I might have told him that."

"And your guy from Des Moines came to see me at work today. He said he didn't mind about the head lice and the toenail fungus."

"You didn't give him my address, did you? I never really was into him."

"You have to stop the catfishing."

"I see that. It was getting old anyway."

"Get in touch with Kenny and tell him you were fibbing and offer to pay for the flowers and candy."

"How about if I tell him we died?" Grandma said.

"No!"

I helped with the dishes after dinner, watched television with everyone for an hour, and took off for home. Ordinarily I would have driven straight to Hamilton, but tonight I wound through the Burg and ended up in front of Morelli's house. Lights were on and I could see the flicker of the television. I sat there for a while feeling connected in a sad kind of way. Then I was connected in an angry kind of way. And ultimately I drove away and gave him the finger. Maybe I should check out Kenny. At least he pays attention to birthdays.

I told Lula I would pick her up at nine-thirty. It was a nice night out, warm for this time of the year, and Lula was sitting on her porch steps when I drove up.

"What's the plan?" she wanted to know when she got into the car.

"He wants to talk. That's all. I just want you to stand at a distance."

"Like I'm backup in case he decides to go maniac or something."

"Yes."

"Okay, I can do that."

"No shooting."

"You got a real thing about no shooting. You ever think you might be in the wrong profession?"

"Every day. Anyway, Ranger took down Blatzo this morning without drawing his gun."

"Yeah, but we aren't Ranger. And what about the first time we went in to get Blatzo, and you were yelling 'Shoot him, shoot him'?"

"Exactly, and it turned out we didn't need to shoot him. You didn't need a gun."

"That's 'cause I had a dildo. Are you saying I should always carry a dildo?"

"The truth is, you're the worst shot on the planet. The chances of you hitting your target are close to zero."

"Boy, that's hurtful. As it happens I have an eyesight problem."

"I didn't know that. What's wrong with your vision?"

"I can't see real good."

"What about glasses?"

"I got them but they ruin my appearance."

"Are you supposed to wear them when you drive?"

"Only if I want to see things like signs. I can see big things like cars."

"Good grief. Put your glasses on."

Lula searched through her purse, found her glasses, and put them on. They were shocking pink and oversized with rhinestones embedded in the frame. She looked like a black Elton John.

"Wow," I said.

"Is that a good *wow* or a bad *wow*?"

"I don't know. I guess it's a shocked *wow*. Where did you get them?"

"At the mall. They have one of them big eyeglass places there. These are some land of designer glasses."

"Can you see better when you wear them?"

"Yeah, except for the reflection I get from the rhinestones sometimes."

"Maybe you should get a more subtle pair of glasses. Something with less bling."

"What's the point to that?"

"How about contact lenses?"

"I tried them but I couldn't get them in. You gotta stick your finger in your eye. You ever try that? It don't work. I don't know how some people can do it."

Mental note. *Help Lula with vision problem.*

"We're supposed to meet Gobbles in the Windward Dorm parking lot," I said. "Windward Dorm is on the same street as Zeta, but it's a couple buildings away. Leave your glasses on so you can read signs."

Windward was easy to find. Lula could have read the sign without her glasses. It might be glorious inside, but no one had wasted time or money designing the exterior. It was a large two-story chunk of brick and mortar. Windows all in a line. A couple doors. That was it. The lot behind it was small and badly lit. Perfect for a rendezvous with a felon.

I parked at the edge of the lot and killed my lights. My eyes adjusted to the darkness, and I picked out two people standing in the deep shadow thrown by a panel van.

"I think that's Gobbles and Julie by the van," I said to Lula. "Stay here and call for help if it looks like I'm in trouble."

"Gotcha."

I approached them slowly. I didn't want them to panic and run. They were holding hands, probably more scared than I was.

"Where's Lula?" Julie asked.

"She's waiting in the car. I thought you might not want to talk in front of her."

"Thank you," Julie said. "This is difficult."

"I get the part about feeling the deck is stacked against you on the assault charge," I said to Gobbles. "But there's more, right?"

"There's more," Gobbles said, "but it's all in bits and missing pieces."

"Start with Professor Pooka," I said. "How long has he been the Zeta advisor?"

"Not long. No one wanted to be our faculty advisor, and Pooka pulled the short straw. He was appointed by Dean Mintner."

"When did this happen?" I asked him.

"The end of the spring semester. We were on probation and our faculty advisor quit."

"And why does Mintner hate Zeta?"

"Have you seen the movie *Animal House*?"

"Yep."

"Well, we're pretty much patterned after that. It's like all the nuts and misfits rolled downhill and ended up in Zeta."

182

"Okay, I have enough background. Tell me about the real problem."

"When we came back to school this year we decided to do something cool for homecoming. I had the idea to shoot off fireworks, and someone said they should be special and reflect the unique qualities of Zeta. So we decided to make them smell like a fart. Stink bomb fireworks."

I was starting to understand Mintner's problem with Zeta.

"The thing is we couldn't find the exact fireworks we were looking for, and we didn't have a lot of money, so we decided to build our own. It's not like they're complicated. All fireworks have the same basic components. Aaron Becker and I took the project over and started to built some prototypes. Everything went great in the beginning, but we couldn't get enough lift when we added the stink bomb. Pooka wasn't just the Zeta advisor, he was also my faculty advisor, so I asked him for help. His area of expertise is biology, but I knew he built rockets as a hobby. I thought he'd be able to steer us toward a better bursting charge."

"Is it legal to build your own fireworks like that?"

"I don't know. I never thought about it. Anyway, Pooka saw what we were doing and got really excited. He was all on board. He knew how to make the fireworks a lot bigger. And he found a source for a better stink bomb container. It's not like you can put a stink bomb in any old thing. Problem was he took over. He had a special lock put on the cellar door, and Becker, Pooka, and I were the only ones with keys. He said he wanted the fireworks to be a surprise. The thing is, it started out as a fun project and before we knew it Becker and I had a top-secret chore on our hands. We had to do test runs in the middle of the night to make sure everything would work right. We couldn't let any of the other brothers in to take a look. And then Pooka changed out the locks a second time, and Becker and I didn't get keys."

"Why did you let him get away with that?"

"I didn't care about locks and fireworks. It was after I got arrested, and I was scared I was going to jail. And that was when Becker disappeared."

"Tell her more about Becker," Julie said.

"Becker didn't have the jail problems I had, and he didn't like that he didn't have keys to the cellar," Gobbles said. "He was imagining all sorts of horrible things happening down there. Everything from white slavery to illegal immigrants to radioactive rats."

"What did you think was going on?" I asked Gobbles.

"I wasn't sure anything was going on. What I saw was that Pooka was losing it. I thought something had happened that sent him over the edge, and he was getting increasingly paranoid. I told Becker to get out of Pooka's space and let him calm down, but Becker was on a mission to get a key."

"Did he get one?"

"I don't know. He's gone. The locks were changed in the morning and Becker disappeared that night. He sent me a text message saying he had to get away for a while, and that was the last I heard. He hasn't answered any of my texts or calls."

"Did you go to the police?"

"I called Becker at home and talked to his parents. They said I shouldn't worry, that he'd called them and said he was on a field trip, doing research."

"You don't believe it?"

"No, I don't believe it, but I didn't think the police would pay attention to me when Becker's parents weren't worried."

"So you've been in the wind, trying to find Becker?"

"Yes, but it turns out we're not great at playing detective. Mostly we tried to watch Pooka. We broke into his apartment once, but he has an alarm system, and we panicked and ran. He lives in a really crappy apartment. Who would have thought he had an alarm?"

"He has aquariums all over the place," Julie said. "We couldn't figure out what was in them."

"We weren't there long enough to really look," Gobbles said.

"Did you notice anything else unusual?" I asked them.

"His apartment is small," Julie said. "One bedroom, one bathroom, tiny kitchen, living room that was being used as an office. Papers and books stacked all over. Dirty dishes in the sink. It was like the Unabomber lived there."

"We broke in through the back door, and I saw a dead rat in the sink," Gobbles said. "That's about it for his apartment. The alarm went off and we ran through really fast because we were looking for Becker. When Becker wasn't in any of the rooms we left."

"Did you follow Pooka around?"

"As much as was possible," Gobbles said. "He goes to his office. He goes to class. He goes to Zeta. He goes home."

"What does he do when he goes to Zeta?"

"He goes straight to the cellar door. He opens it and disappears into the cellar. An hour later he reappears. He locks up and leaves without talking to anyone. I was worried he might have Becker locked up down there so I had a friend bump the lock and break in."

"What did he find?"

"Fireworks. Pooka still has the fireworks there."

"Have you tried to make contact?"

"I called him once, and he kept asking me where I was hiding. And he tried to get me to meet with him. I was afraid he was going to turn me in."

"I have a friend who has a class with Pooka," Julie said. "She says he rambles on about how bad the school is, and how it squashes creative research. And then she says he scribbles some numbers and symbols on the board and leaves."

"Isn't anyone reporting his behavior?"

"He's not so far off the bubble," Gobbles said. "A lot of the teachers come in and rant on social and political issues and then tell you to go home and read chapter ten."

"And it's not as if Dean Mintner was any more sane," Julie said. "He was obsessed with closing Zeta."

"So where do we go from here?" I asked them.

"I think someone needs to see what's happening in the Zeta house cellar," Gobbles said. "It has to be more than fireworks. And I wouldn't mind knowing what was in those aquariums."

"I don't want to know about the contents of the aquariums," Julie said. "Don't anyone tell me."

"Right now you're a felon," I said to Gobbles. "Would you like me to check you in with the court and get you bailed out again?"

"No. I'm afraid the judge might not set bail, and I'll be locked away, and Becker won't be able to get in touch with me."

"Be careful," I said to Gobbles. "Go hide somewhere and let me figure this out."

I couldn't believe I was saying this. Stephanie Plum, total screwup, worst bounty hunter ever . . . and I was going to solve the mystery of the cellar and find Becker.

I walked back to Lula and slid behind the wheel.

"So how'd that go?" Lula asked.

"It's complicated."

CHAPTER
TWENTY

The bonds office is open for half a day on Saturdays, but I work all the time. It's not a big sacrifice for me because I have no hobbies, I don't play any sports, and I no longer have a boyfriend. As a special Saturday treat I skipped breakfast at home and got coffee and a cruller at Dunkin' Donuts. Lula and Connie were already at the office when I strolled in.

"What are we going to do today?" Lula asked me. "Are we going looking for bad guys?"

"I'm going to Rangeman to ask Ranger for help with the Gobbles dilemma."

"That could be why you're wearing a tight low-cut shirt that shows off your boobies," Lula said. "And you got on the tight skinny jeans. And you got on makeup."

"I always dress like this."

"No way. Half the time you can't tell if you buy your clothes in the men's department or the women's department. You're one of them comfortable dressers."

"She has a point," Connie said. "You haven't got your hair in a ponytail today, either."

"Jeez," I said. "I hadn't really thought about any of that. I just get up every morning and get dressed."

"Exactly," Lula said, "but today you got dressed special. This here's your unconscious telling you to get sexed up for Mr Tall, Dark, and Totally Edible. Let's face it. You're hot for him."

"Of course I'm hot for him," I said. "You'd have to be dead not to be hot for him. That doesn't mean I'm setting out to seduce him."

"Well, I'm just saying you got seduction cleavage going on," Lula said. "And I'm thinking your unconscious has plans."

"As long as those plans stay in my unconscious," I said. I tossed my empty coffee cup into the trash. "I'm off to Rangeman."

I texted Ranger from the car to make sure he had time to talk to me, and he texted back *Babe*. I took that to mean he had time.

I parked in the underground garage and took the elevator to the third-floor control room where Ranger had an office. When Ranger got out of the military he worked as a bounty hunter with a vacant lot for an address. In a relatively short amount of time he went from a vacant lot to a slick office building, an exclusive client base, and a fleet of new cars. He has a silent partner who remains very silent. The control room is state of the art. The decor is minimalist. The attitude is calm and quiet.

I walked through the control room to Ranger's office. The door was open, and Ranger was working at his computer. I closed the door and took a seat across the desk from him.

"Catching up on Facebook?" I asked him.

"Designing a security system."

"I had an interesting chat with Ken Globovic last night. Long story short is that Gobbles and his friend Becker were building fireworks in the basement of Zeta house. Professor Pooka came on board to help and totally took over. He has the basement door locked, and he has the only key. No one gets in the basement but Pooka. I'm told Pooka lives in an apartment like the Unabomber, and that it has an alarm system. And Becker has been missing for over a week. Gobbles has been FTA because he's trying to find Becker."

"No police involvement?"

"Becker called his parents and assured them that he was fine."

"But Gobbles doesn't think Becker is fine."

"Right."

"Why do we care?"

"I don't know. I just care."

Ranger looked at me for a beat. "I like your shirt."

"It's working, right?"

"Not as good as the red dress, but it's close. What do you want me to do?"

"I want to see what's in the Zeta cellar and Pooka's apartment."

"I'm assuming we don't want Pooka in his apartment when we look at it."

"Correct. I can arrange to have him out when we're going in, but there's the alarm."

"I can manage the alarm. Just give me the address."

"You're going to hack his alarm?"

"Not me personally."

I texted Gobbles and told him to get Pooka out of his apartment and to send me the address. I got an answer back in less than five minutes. Gobbles was meeting Pooka at a Starbucks in a half hour. The address he gave me for Pooka's apartment was close to Kiltman.

Ranger made a phone call and passed the address on, asking for a two-hour window. I assumed this was to his hacker, who for all I knew could be in China.

"Let's roll," Ranger said. "I have afternoon client meetings."

I stood and he gave me a slow full-body scan, taking in the skinny jeans.

"Babe, you must want more than two simple breakins."

I smiled at him. "Maybe."

Holy cats. Was I flirting with Ranger? This was all Lula's fault.

We took the elevator to the garage, and Ranger chose to drive my Macan. The Macan was like a stealth Porsche. It flew under the radar and didn't draw the attention of Ranger's 911 Turbo.

Pooka lived in a large house that had been subdivided into four apartments. His apartment was on the second floor and ran front to back. He had his own outside entrance at the rear of the house, plus an interior entrance that opened off the front door. He was two blocks from the Kiltman campus and three blocks from the Starbucks where he was going to meet Gobbles. It was a Saturday morning and traffic was minimal.

Ranger parked across the street and one house down. Julie was going to call us when Pooka walked into the Starbucks, but it wasn't necessary because we saw Pooka leave his house. He exited through the front door and turned left. We watched him walk a block and turn left again.

We crossed the street, walked into the house as if we owned it, and took the stairs to Pooka's apartment. Ranger tried the door. Locked. He took a slim pick from his pocket and opened the door. No alarm.

We stepped in, closed the door, and stood for a couple beats taking it all in. It was like a hoarder was conducting mad scientist lab experiments. Small aquariums stacked three tall lined a kitchen counter. There were more of them in the room that was designed to be a living room but was now a strange office and lab.

He had a large scarred wood desk that held stacks of papers, crumpled fast food bags, cigarettes stubbed out in used coffee cups, a small digital food scale, and a place for a computer, but the computer was missing.

The single bedroom contained more aquariums, more stacks of papers, and an unmade bed. The ratty quilt on the bed had ink stains and cigarette burns on it. More crumpled fast food bags and discarded Starbucks coffee cups.

I took a closer look at the aquariums and broke out in goosebumps. They were filled with tiny bugs. Every aquarium.

"What are these?" I asked Ranger.

192

"I'm not an expert, but they look like fleas," Ranger said. "I imagine he's breeding them for use in an experiment."

No surprises in the bathroom. It was filthy as expected. The medicine chest was crammed with sleep aids, decongestants, pill bottles without labels, Benadryl, and a variety of prescription meds.

Kitchen cabinets were filled with screw-capped jars holding powdered chemicals. Some were labeled and some weren't. One whole cabinet was devoted to small empty glass vials with stoppers. Mixed in with the powdered chemicals was a box of Cheerios and a jar of peanut butter.

He had a pint of chocolate ice cream and a bag of frozen mice in his freezer. The refrigerator contained a half gallon of milk, and what appeared to be a bag of blood.

There were assorted devices on a small kitchen table that a biologist or chemist might use. A Bunsen burner, a couple glass flasks, a suction device, and there were furry black spots of something growing in a petri dish.

"I'm completely grossed out," I said to Ranger. "How can anyone live in here?"

"I want to take a quick look at some of these stacks of papers. While I'm doing that I'd like you to document the apartment. Go through and take pictures of the fleas and the equipment and the medicine chest."

We'd been in the apartment for exactly a half hour when we got a call from Julie saying Pooka was on his way home.

"I'm sorry," she said. "We couldn't keep him here any longer. He wanted Gobbles to go home with him, and when Gobbles refused he got angry and stomped off."

"It's okay," I said. "Thanks for the heads-up."

Ranger and I took the back door out, crossed into the neighboring yard, and returned to the Macan.

"Next stop the Zeta house," Ranger said.

"Take the loop road through the campus and turn when you see Windward Dorm. Zeta is a couple buildings down from Windward." I buckled myself in. "Did you find anything interesting in all those stacks of papers?"

"Some of them looked like student term papers. Most of them were copies of professional articles. I don't know enough biology to understand the content. His doctoral thesis was bound and on his desk. There were a couple professional journals on his desk. He had pages that mentioned him earmarked."

Ranger turned onto the loop road, found Zeta, and parked in the small lot at the side of the building.

"I've never seen the campus this quiet," I said. "No one's picketing Zeta. No one's playing Frisbee. No music blasting out. No one's on the porch yelling sexist slurs at the women passing by. No women passing by."

"Saturday morning," Ranger said.

The inside of Zeta was just as quiet. No music. No television. A couple brothers stumbled past us on the way to the kitchen.

"We're invisible," I said to Ranger, leading him to the cellar door. "Probably everyone is still blind drunk from last night."

194

Ranger looked at the two locks that had been installed on the door. "No problem here."

Moments later the door was open and we stepped inside. Ranger locked us in and flipped the lights on. The Zeta basement was one large room that had been finished at a basic utilitarian level. Cement floor, raw drywall ceiling and walls. No-frills fluorescent lighting. Mechanicals were at the far end of the room. Cases of soda and water were stacked back by the mechanicals. There were several empty kegs by the cases of soda.

Two large folding tables had been set up in the middle of the room directly under one of the lights, and paper tubes were lined up on the tables. A box of firecrackers had been set to the side on the floor. A bunch of empty red and silver tins had been tossed into a big box. Another box held tins that hadn't been opened.

"Fireworks," I said.

"I know something about fireworks and these aren't typical. Besides the usual components these are designed to hold a containment package."

"A stink bomb?"

"Not likely. The odor would disperse too quickly."

"What then?"

"I don't know. I don't see anything unusual here that he might want to put inside the shell."

"Was there anything in his apartment?"

"Fleas," Ranger said.

"What would he do with the fleas?"

"How crazy is this professor? Is he terrorist crazy?"

"I don't know," I said. "I've had limited contact. He's angry. Doesn't seem to like the school. I know from Monica Linken that he was turned down for tenure and his research was defunded."

"When I was going through the papers I found several articles on Unit 731 and aerial dispersion of pathogens."

"What's Unit 731?"

"It was a unit of the Japanese Imperial Army during World War II. It was engaged in covert biological and chemical warfare research and development. I'm mentioning this because the articles were on Pooka's desk, and not warehoused in a stack in a corner. I didn't read through the articles, so I don't know if they're relevant, but I know that one of the Unit 731 projects involved bubonic plague and fleas. The Japanese army infected fleas with the plague and dropped them from planes on the Chinese countryside. Supposedly they killed thousands of people. Maybe hundreds of thousands."

"Omigod. Pooka's fleas. Do you think he's planning on dropping plague-infected fleas at homecoming?"

"Not sure where he'd get plague, but he has a lot of fleas. Someone would have to be really sick to disseminate plague."

I was looking at the red and silver tins. "What are these?"

"Blasting grade black powder. It's used as a bursting charge. Pooka isn't much of a housekeeper. He's obviously spilled some on the floor and not cleaned it up. You don't want to light a match around this stuff. Be careful not to step in it."

I pulled my phone out and called Morelli.

"I found the black powder," I said. "Meet me at the Zeta house."

CHAPTER
TWENTY-ONE

Ranger stayed until Morelli arrived and then he took off, picked up by one of his patrolmen. Morelli stood hands on hips, looking around the cellar.

"Fireworks," he said. "The lab should have picked up on that. This is blasting powder. Gun enthusiasts use a different grade."

"Pooka is the only one with a key to the cellar," I told Morelli.

"How did you and Ranger get in?"

"I suspected Gobbles might be down here, so we let ourselves in. I also suspected Gobbles might be in Pooka's apartment so we let ourselves in there, too."

Morelli looked like he was in pain. "Do I want to know this?"

"For you to decide. I have pictures."

"Body parts in the fridge?" he asked.

"Blood."

"What?"

"He had a bag that looked like it contained blood in his refrigerator. And he had dead mice in his freezer. I think he was feeding it to his fleas."

"Fleas. Why doesn't he just get his fleas a dog like everyone else?"

"He's *raising* the fleas. He's got aquariums all over his apartment, and they're filled with fleas."

"You're making this up."

"I swear." I gave him my phone. "Thumb through the pictures."

"This is Pooka's apartment?"

"Pictures don't do it justice. You can't smell pictures."

"Here's my problem," Morelli said. "All this might prove is that the murder victims were in this cellar. I have nothing that connects it to the murder weapon."

"Do you know about Unit 731?"

"Yes. The Japanese army had a facility where they performed horrible acts in the name of science."

"And they dropped fleas that were contaminated with bubonic plague on the Chinese," I said.

"Did you see any vials of bubonic plague in Pooka's apartment?"

"No, but some of the vials weren't labeled."

Even as I said it I felt like an idiot. I mean, the whole thing was too bizarre and hard to believe.

"Was that a serious question?" I asked Morelli.

"I think so, but it's so far-fetched I'm almost embarrassed I asked it."

"The fireworks Pooka was building have a place to put a little canister of something or other," I said. "Originally it was supposed to be a stink bomb, but the plan might have gotten changed, and maybe he was planning on exploding fleas over the campus at homecoming."

"Oh boy."

"Why else would he be raising fleas?"

"No clue," Morelli said. "Maybe there's a market for fleas, and he's selling them on eBay. Maybe they're pets. Maybe they're used for scientific experiments."

Morelli examined the shells that were lined up on the table.

"There are two different setups here," he said. "I can see where one has a place for a canister. I don't know about exploding fleas, but at the very least this is illegal. You can't manufacture, store, or transport fireworks in New Jersey without a permit. And I don't see any permits displayed. I'm shutting this down, and I'll bring someone in to take a look at it, and clean it out."

A half hour later, the area was secured by two uniforms, and a munitions guy was at work.

"Are you going to take a look at his apartment?" I asked Morelli.

"I'm going to question him and list him as a person of interest, but I can't go into his apartment. It's not like I'm a bounty hunter with blanket permission. I have to go to a judge before I can get in."

"Would you like me to go back in?"

"No! I have enough problems. I'm drinking Prilosec by the gallons. You're like Calamity Jane. I'm afraid you'll come out of there with the plague."

"So you think he might be harboring plague-infected fleas?"

"No. I was making a point." He checked his watch. "You want to go to lunch?"

"Sure."

We went to a deli that was a block from the school and sat at one of the small outside tables.

"You look nice," Morelli said. "Are you going someplace special?"

"Turning over a new leaf."

"I thought the old leaf was pretty good."

"Thanks. I'll probably be back to the old leaf tomorrow."

I ordered a ham and cheese panini, and Morelli ordered cottage cheese.

"You're going to get kicked out of Trenton for ordering cottage cheese," I said.

"I don't know what to eat. Everything bothers me."

"Have you seen a doctor?"

"Yeah. He has stomach problems, too. So what are you going to do about Globovic? I get the feeling you're not working too hard to bring him in."

"There's a complication. Globovic was working with a guy named Becker to make fireworks for homecoming. They ran into some problems and asked Pooka to help them, and Pooka took over. Globovic got arrested and shortly after that Becker went missing and hasn't been seen since. Globovic is FTA because he's trying to find Becker."

"Why hasn't anyone reported this to the police?"

"Globovic doesn't think the police will pay attention to him because Becker called his parents and told them he was fine."

"What do *you* think?" Morelli asked me.

"I think there's something bad going on. Three men are dead and Becker is missing."

"You realize this isn't your job, right? You're not on the payroll to save the world?"

"So then who's supposed to save the world?"

"Good point," Morelli said. "For sure not me. I need a bathroom. I'll be right back."

Gobbles called while Morelli was away.

"How did it go?" he asked. "Did you find anything in his apartment? I heard you got into the Zeta cellar and the police are there now."

"His apartment was just as you described it. The aquariums were filled with fleas."

"That makes sense. We were just starting to build the new models, and we all had flea bites. Pooka said he probably brought them in. That he'd been having flea problems in his apartment. It was the first week of school, and we were having an alum mixer, and Harry Getz was there. So Becker asked Getz to send someone around to get rid of the fleas."

"Why Getz?" I asked.

"He owns an extermination company. Actually I guess it's construction, but they do exterminating, too. He was partners with another Zeta alum, Doug Linken, and the company was in the toilet."

"And did he get rid of the fleas?"

"Yeah. Some guy came and sprayed the cellar."

"Did Getz ever go into the cellar?"

"Yeah, he came back to check on the fleas and Becker took him down. That was when the three of us had keys. Getz saw that we were building fireworks and didn't like it. Said it was a fire hazard, and we needed

202

to clean it out. He said he was going to have a talk with Pooka."

"What day was that?"

"It was the day Getz got shot. He was at Zeta around lunchtime, and he was shot that night. It was a Wednesday, and then Becker disappeared the next day, and Pooka had the locks changed a second time."

"Do you suppose Pooka shot Getz?"

"Why would he do that? Over fireworks? That's not a good reason to shoot someone."

Not if you're sane.

"I'll be back in touch," I said. "Let me know if you hear from Becker."

"I was hoping he was in the cellar," Gobbles said. "And alive."

I disconnected and Morelli came back.

"You look kind of white," I said to him.

"Just the thought of food has my intestines in a knot."

"That's serious."

"It's probably some stupid virus."

The waitress set our food down and Morelli went from white to green.

"How long has this been going on?" I asked him.

"I don't know. A month maybe. Maybe two months."

"You never said anything."

"Look at me. I'm macho man. We don't talk about stuff like that. It screws with our hotness. Cramping and diarrhea aren't on the checklist of ways to get laid." He poked at his cottage cheese. "I think I'm getting old. My Uncle Baldy talks about this stuff, and he's a hundred."

"Jeez, Morelli, you have a house and a dog and a toaster. I thought you were past the Italian Stallion thing. I thought you had some level of maturity."

"There's a difference between *having* maturity and being *mature*. I'm not ready to be mature. I don't want to see the AARP magazine in my mailbox."

Morelli's phone buzzed with a text message. "I have to go," he said. "They want me back at the fraternity."

"You didn't have anything to eat. Do you want half my sandwich?"

"Thanks, but I'm supposed to be off gluten. I can't eat bread."

"Pizza?"

"Dead to me."

"Birthday cake?"

"Gone from my life."

"Is it working?"

"No."

I finished my lunch and headed for home. Morelli had always seemed invincible to me. He waded through crap every day and it all washed off in the shower. Even as a kid he was constantly getting into trouble and landing on his feet. He broke his leg and he was fine. He was shot and he was fine. Never defeated. And now he was the victim of cramping and diarrhea and he wasn't sounding good. It was so atypical for Morelli that it was hard for me to wrap my head around it.

I was still thinking about Morelli when I got to my apartment building. Maybe he was right to reach the conclusion that the stress of the job had finally gotten to him. And having a Calamity Jane girlfriend added to the stress. So he was cutting us out of his life. I guess I couldn't blame him. I might do the same. Not sure I'd want a relationship with someone who gave me cramps.

I parked, took the elevator to the second floor, and found a man sitting in front of my door. He jumped up when he saw me. Excited. All smiley. Not a big guy. Maybe five five. In his thirties. Thinning sandy blond hair. Looked like he never spent a day in the sun. Dress slacks and a blue dress shirt tucked in. Red suspenders.

"Gina Bigelow!" he said. "I'd know you anywhere. We finally meet."

Just when you think your day can't possibly get any more bizarre . . . it does.

"Let me guess," I said. "Kenny."

He reached out for me. "Do I dare kiss you hello?"

"No. If you take one step closer I'll zap you with my stun gun."

"Hah. I knew you'd be a great kidder."

"There's been a misunderstanding. I'm not the person you've been talking to online. Do you know what it means to be catfished?"

"Yes."

"Well, you've been catfished. Someone used my picture without my permission."

"That's terrible." He thought about it for a beat and got all smiley again. "It doesn't matter. Here you are

205

and here I am and it's perfect. It was meant to be. It was fate that brought us together."

"It wasn't fate. It was my grandmother. I'm sorry for your inconvenience but you're going to have to leave. I have things to do."

"What sort of things?"

"Just *things*."

"I could do them with you."

"No!"

"Would you like to have dinner with me? I'll take you someplace nice."

"No."

"It's the least you could do. I've spent a lot of time on this. And I've put in a certain amount of effort."

"How about you have dinner with my grandmother?"

"I don't think so. I think I deserve dinner with you."

"Why me?" I asked. "Why do these things happen to me?"

"I guess you're lucky," he said. "I'll come back at six o'clock. Do you like seafood?"

"No."

"Would you like a kitten? My cat just had kittens."

"Thank you, but no. I have a hamster."

I watched him leave, and I let myself into my apartment. Good God, I thought. I had a date. Just shoot me.

At five-thirty I dragged myself over to my closet and tried to muster up some enthusiasm for dressing for dinner. I didn't want to wear anything sexy or, for that matter, mildly attractive. I settled on black slacks, a simple white shirt, the red jacket, and flats. I was debating if this date was worth makeup when Gobbles called on my cellphone.

"We've been watching Pooka," Gobbles said. "He just went to Zeta and freaked. We weren't even close to him, and we could hear him going apeshit. He was demanding to know who had violated his private space. That was his exact word. *Violated*."

"Were the police still there?"

"No. From what I hear they cleaned the place out and have crime scene tape across the cellar door. Pooka was completely gonzo. He was waving his arms and ranting. He kept asking who was responsible. It's possible that your name was mentioned. Like I said, we were at a distance and couldn't hear everything, but you should be extra careful. He's really nuts."

"Thanks. I'll put my bulletproof vest on."

"Do you really have one?"

"No."

"Too bad," Gobbles said.

I hung up and decided the night was worth one swipe of mascara and some lip gloss.

A little before six someone rapped on my door. Kenny is early, I thought. And my guess is he was always early. He had *premature ejaculator* written all over him. I opened the door and Pooka burst in.

"You!" he said. "You brought the police to my workroom. How dare you? You ruined everything. It was all in place. Justice was going to be served. And you destroyed it. Now I have to start over. It won't be as spectacular, but I'll succeed. And you'll pay. You're on the list. You're at the top. I would kill you now but that would be too easy for you. I want you to live with fear. I want you to know a horrible death is in your future."

"They were just fireworks."

"Not just fireworks. Those fireworks were an elegant delivery system. They would have brought joy and then horror. You've delayed the inevitable, but my mission will go forward. This institution must be destroyed. It will be a symbol of the evil it represents. No one will set foot on this soil for a century. It will be the Chernobyl of academia."

"Is this about tenure?" I asked. "I could put in a good word for you."

"Really?" He shook his head. "No. I won't be swayed. Tenure is the work of the devil." His hand went to the amulet. "We won't be tricked into passivity by empty promises."

"We? Let me take a wild guess here. Does the amulet talk to you?"

"It guides me."

"Have you ever thought about seeing a healthcare professional? I could find someone who would help you better understand the power of the amulet."

"Healthcare is just another way of allowing employers and the government to control you. What's the first thing they do when you step into a doctor's office? They take your clothes. It's a power grab. A naked man has no power."

Clearly he doesn't know Ranger.

"So what does the amulet think about all the fleas?" I asked him.

"You know about the fleas? How could you know about the fleas?" He had a grip on the amulet, and red spots had popped out on his cheeks. "What else do you know?"

"I know about Unit 731."

I was taking a winger here, but I thought why not? Throw it out and see if it goes somewhere.

"A hideous misuse of scientific experiment," Pooka said. "The primary function of that program was to satisfy the prurient needs of a man who couldn't get an erection."

"I hadn't heard about that part."

"It's blatantly obvious. The program could have been brilliant, but it was mired in sadomasochistic gratification."

"Okay. Whatever."

"That wasn't even the most egregious part. It was all so crude and unimaginative. And they had wonderful pathogens like the plague, and they disseminated it in clay pots. *Clay pots!* Shame on them. The plague deserves better."

"The plague deserves fireworks."

"Yes!"

I was trying to look like I was really into this, but my skin had the creepy crawlies and had broken out in goosebumps.

Kenny came up behind Pooka.

"Here I am," Kenny said. "Right on time. I'm very punctual."

Pooka turned to him. "Who is this?"

"He's sort of my date," I said. "By the way, did you kill Harry Getz?"

"There are no answers," Pooka said. "There are only questions."

He whirled around and left, taking the stairs.

"Who was that?" Kenny asked. "He was wearing pajamas."

"It's complicated."

By eight o'clock Kenny and I decided we had nothing in common. He ordered an appletini and I had beer. He ate sushi and I had a burger. He watched PBS and I watched ESPN.

He dropped me off at my door and asked if I'd stun gun him if he tried to kiss me. I said *yes*, and he shook my hand and left.

CHAPTER
TWENTY-TWO

I was lying in bed wondering if I should just stay there all day, and a text message came in. It was from Lula saying she thinks my doorbell must be broken, because she's at my door, and I'm not opening it.

I dragged myself out of bed and opened the door for her.

"You look like you just woke up," Lula said.

"I had a horrible night. I couldn't sleep. I kept thinking about fleas and plague. What time is it?"

"It's almost ten o'clock. I just came from church, and I thought I'd stop in and find out about yesterday's events."

"You go to church?"

"Of course I go to church. I gotta compensate for all the things I do that would otherwise send me straight to hell."

I went to the kitchen and got coffee going.

"Do you believe in God?" I asked Lula.

"Fuckin' A I believe in God. Don't you believe in God?"

"I believe in something. It's vague."

"You should come with me next week. I go to the Baptist church on State Street."

"I'm Catholic."

"That's okay. We don't care. Nobody's perfect. Us Baptists say the more the merrier. We do some praying and singing and we praise the Lord. I'm all about the Lord. Especially on a Sunday morning."

I put two frozen waffles in the toaster.

"That's a new toaster," Lula said.

"Morelli gave it to me. He used to like to have toast in the morning."

"So tell me about yesterday. Last I saw you was when you were going over to see Ranger and you were all sexed up."

"Ranger got me into Pooka's apartment and the Zeta cellar."

"How'd that go?"

"Pooka's apartment is disgusting. He's breeding fleas in aquariums, and he's got a bag of blood in his refrigerator."

"Say what?"

"I have no proof but I think Pooka might have intended to load the fireworks up with fleas and drop the fleas on the Kiltman campus."

"Why's he want to give everybody fleas?"

"Not sure."

I couldn't shake the possibility of plague, but I didn't want to start a riot by telling Lula. I poured coffee for us, and we each took a waffle.

"You got maple syrup for this?" Lula asked.

"No."

"Strawberry compote?"

"No."

212

"What do you put on it?"

"I just eat it. I'm usually in a hurry."

Gobbles called on my cellphone. "I started watching Pooka at six o'clock this morning just like always. You could set your clock by him seven days a week. He comes out at seven and goes to his office. He stays there until noon. Only he didn't come out today. And then ten minutes ago he parked in front of his house in a junker van. He went in and immediately came out carrying a cardboard box. He went back in and got two aquariums, loaded it all in the back of the van, and took off. I couldn't follow him. I haven't got a car. Do you think I should break into his apartment? I think he's moving out."

"Wait for me. I'll be right over."

"What's up?" Lula asked.

"It looks like Pooka is moving stuff out of his apartment."

"The one with the fleas?"

"I need to get dressed. Put my coffee in a travel mug and give Rex a couple Cheerios. I'll be right out."

We took Lula's car and made good time going across town. Not a lot of traffic on Sunday morning. Pooka's street was quiet. Gobbles stepped from the side of a building when we parked.

"He hasn't been back," Gobbles said. "I went inside to take a look about five minutes ago and his door was locked."

"How did you break in last time?" I asked him.

"I bumped the lock on the back door. I wouldn't have done it, but I was hoping Becker was in there. I thought Pooka might have been holding Becker as a hostage. Or I guess I was half-afraid I'd find something awful."

"What made you suspect Pooka?"

"Becker just had this feeling about Pooka. He spent more time with him than I did, and he thought he was creepy. And then when the lock got changed the second time, Becker was convinced there was something bad going on. When he disappeared I figured either he was afraid of Pooka or Pooka did something to him."

"Let's do it," Lula said. "Let's scope this place out."

I didn't totally share her enthusiasm. I was a teensy bit worried that there'd be fleas jumping around and they'd be shot full of bubonic plague. I was willing to peek inside and see if anybody was home, but at the first sign of a flea I was turning the project over to the hazmat team.

We trudged up to the second floor and knocked on Pooka's door. No answer. The door was locked.

"Doesn't look like much of a lock," Lula said.

She took a screwdriver out of her purse, inserted it into the lock, hit the screwdriver with the butt of her gun, and the door popped open.

We cautiously looked inside.

"*Yoo-hoo*," Lula called. "Anybody home?"

Nothing. We crept in and moved through the rooms. I didn't see any fleas. Not on the floor. Not in aquariums. The aquariums were all gone. No blood or mice in the refrigerator. No dead rats in the sink.

"I don't think he's coming back," Lula said. "On account of he cleaned up. He's got one of those bags

214

that you see in the hospital holding blood and shit and it's empty and in the garbage. It's got writing on it. It says *Yersinia pestis*. Is that someone's name?"

I googled it on my iPhone. It was the bacteria responsible for bubonic plague.

"Don't touch it," I said. "Everyone out. Now. Don't stop until you're on the sidewalk."

I stomped my feet and checked myself over to make sure I didn't have any fleas on me, and I called Morelli.

"I'm sorry to bother you," I said. "I know it's Sunday, and you're not feeling great, but I think you'll want to see this. And bring a hazmat suit."

"Seriously?"

"Seriously."

I gave him the address and told him about the empty bag in the garbage.

"I feel itchy all over," Lula said. "I think I got a flea on me. And what if he's got some of that *Yersinia* stuff in him? That can't be good, right?"

"Yeah," I said. "It wouldn't be good."

"Of course I just came from church, so I might still have some holy protection."

Gobbles wasn't saying anything. He had a grim set to his mouth, and I knew he had it figured out.

"There are going to be police here," I said to Gobbles. "You might want to go home or wherever it is that you go."

"You'll call me?"

"As soon as I know something."

"So let me see if I got this put together right," Lula said. "Pooka was making fleas, and he was gonna shoot them off in the fireworks. And then all the people at homecoming would get fleas dropped on them, and the fleas might be infected with this *Yersinia*. Which we don't want to have, either."

"Right."

"And just exactly what is this *Yersinia?*" She tapped it into her phone. "*Plague!*" she yelled. "It's freaking plague. It's the black death. Do you know what this shit does to you? It gives you boo-boos. And then your fingers and toes turn black and fall off. Good thing I don't have a dick. Imagine what it could do to that!" She kicked her shoes off and looked at her toes. "I see a flea. I got a flea on me. Shoot it. Burn it. Somebody do something."

I looked down at her feet. "I don't see any fleas."

"What's that on my big toe?"

"It looks like a wart."

"Oh yeah, I forgot. I have to go home," Lula said. "I'm gonna take a shower and boil all my clothes. If I leave can you catch a ride with Morelli?"

"No problem."

I was alone when Morelli pulled to the curb.

"I have a hazmat team on the way," he said. "Do you know if anyone's in the house?"

"I haven't seen anyone. I have a description of Pooka's van but no license plate number. You probably want to sift through his office in the science building."

A patrol car arrived and parked beside Morelli's SUV, and Morelli gave the uniform instructions to secure the second-floor apartment but not go in.

"We don't want this broadcast on the evening news," Morelli said. "Who knows about this besides you?"

"Gobbles. And he's not going to say anything. And Lula. She just went home to boil her clothes."

I saw sweat bead on Morelli's upper lip.

"Cramps?" I asked him.

"It's okay. It'll pass. Probably. We need to contain Lula. I don't suppose you'd be willing to babysit her for a couple days."

"What all would that involve?"

"Twenty-four-seven. You could bring her over to your apartment."

"Are you insane? Live with Lula? She snores. *Loud*. And she would be in my bathroom. I don't like other people in my bathroom."

"You let me use it."

"I didn't mind you using it. It felt *friendly*. I was in love with you."

"I notice you used the past tense. You're not still in love with me?"

"I am but I don't want to admit it. And I certainly don't want to say it out loud."

"I'd kiss you, but I have cramps," Morelli said.

A hazmat van rumbled up and parked.

"This is going to be a long day," Morelli said. "If it turns out the bag of plague is for real, this place will be crawling with every three-letter agency in the country."

"I'd go home and clean my hamster cage, but I don't have a car."

Morelli gave me his keys. "Take my SUV. I'll pick it up when I'm done here."

"Can I bring you a yogurt or something?"

"No, but thanks. I'm off dairy."

"Is there anything left that you can eat?"

"Alcohol, as long as it's not made with grain."

I put Rex in the bathtub while I cleaned his cage. I returned him to the cage and scrubbed the bathroom. I vacuumed the floors, dusted the few things that collected dust, washed the kitchen floor, and took the garbage out to the trash chute. My mother and grandmother seem to get satisfaction from this. I get nothing. I would get satisfaction from paying a housekeeper once a week to clean my house. Unfortunately I'm not in that income bracket. I'm almost in the no income bracket.

Morelli showed up at three-thirty.

"Do you need to use the bathroom?" I asked him.

"No, but it's comforting to know there's one close by."

"I'd offer you something to eat, but I don't think I have anything."

"It's okay. I just had a gluten-free, dairy-free snack bar that tasted like sawdust. I'm going to go home and eat half a loaf of gluten-free, dairy-free bread. I think I can put grape jelly on it."

"Can you eat chicken? We could make a roast chicken."

"You know how to roast a chicken?"

"Almost. My mother roasts chickens all the time."

"I appreciate the offer but I think I'll go home and stick with the bread. The good news is that Becker might be alive and with Pooka. The bad news is that he might not be in great shape. It turns out that Pooka doesn't just rent that apartment. He actually owns the house and rents out the other three units. At the back end of the property there's a single-car garage where he's been keeping the white van. The van isn't there anymore but he's left behind a load of garbage. Without going into gruesome detail, we've collected evidence that would indicate someone was being kept in the garage. It looks like he was sedated and restrained and either giving blood or getting blood. My guess is he was *giving* blood and that Pooka was using it to feed his fleas. Nothing has been analyzed yet, so this is all conjecture. Some of the containers left behind were labeled and some weren't, so we don't know exactly what we're seeing. The bag in the garbage in the apartment is being looked at by the CDC. We're going on the assumption that it's real."

"I thought plague was eradicated."

"Not entirely. A small number of cases pop up every year. It can be treated with antibiotics, but it's still life threatening and it's an ugly disease. And it wouldn't be impossible for someone to get hold of an infected rat or even a rogue vial. Pooka is a biology professor. I imagine he knows how to get his hands on all sorts of stuff."

"That's scary."

"Yes. And it's now considered domestic terrorism, so along with the FBI, the CDC, and the state police, we have Homeland Security digging around in every garbage receptacle from here to Camden. I'm happy about it because I'm out of the plague business. All I have to do is solve three murders."

"Sorry I dragged you into this."

"You didn't drag me in. I was dragged in when I pulled the first homicide. And, honestly, I'd be all about this if I didn't feel so lousy."

"Don't worry about Lula. She's home and she's busy doing laundry. I'll see her first thing in the morning, and I'll take control."

"I expect it's no longer an issue. We have guys running around in biohazard suits. The only thing missing from the circus is a detonation robot. The SAT truck cruised in just as I was leaving."

I watched Morelli walk down the hall, I closed my door, and locked all three of my locks. This still didn't make me feel entirely safe. I'd been threatened with a horrible death by a lunatic who'd most likely already killed three people. All it would take was a single infected flea. It could hop under my door. It could sit in the hallway and wait for me to walk to the elevator. And just like that I'd have bubonic plague. At least my apartment was clean. If I got the plague my mother wouldn't be embarrassed about my housekeeping.

CHAPTER
TWENTY-THREE

It was Monday morning, and I had to go to the office. I looked out my security peephole into the hall. No lunatics in sight. I stepped out and studied the carpet. No fleas hopping around. If there were fleas on the carpet they were sleeping in. Best to try to forget about the fleas.

Connie was alone in the office when I walked in. Vinnie's door was shut, and I didn't see his car parked outside. No Lula.

"Where is everybody?" I asked Connie.

"Vinnie is at the courthouse, and Lula is always late. It's just that you're usually later than Lula. Sounds like you had a fun day yesterday. I saw the guys in the hazmat suits on the evening news. We made national again."

"Did they say anything about fleas?"

"No. They said there was the rumor of biological warfare by a terrorist cell. And they showed a picture of Pooka that made him look totally insane."

"At least they got that right."

The door crashed open, and Lula bustled in. "We were on the evening news *and* the morning news. I couldn't get unglued from my television."

"*We?*" I asked.

"Trenton," Lula said. "They didn't get a whole lot about the situation right, but there was a picture of Pooka that if it was me I'd rush out and get a makeover."

I squinted across the room at her. "What have you got around your neck? Omigod, is that a flea collar?"

"Damn skippy it's a flea collar. I'm not taking no chances. Suppose that nutcase Pooka decides to go spreading his fleas everywhere. Or he could be building new fireworks even as we speak." Lula tapped her head with her index finger. "No grass growin' here. I'm no dummy. I went out and got myself some flea protection. This here's the size for a big dog."

"It's got sparldy jewels in it," Connie said.

"I bedazzled it," Lula said. "It's practical and yet it's fashionable. I might go into business making these. There's a lot of people out there with flea issues. Even if your fleas don't have plague, you still don't want them sucking out your blood, right?"

"Plague?" Connie asked.

"She didn't say plague," I said. "She said *plaque* like in heart disease."

"Holy Mary, Mother of God," Connie said. "Are you shitting me? *Plague?* Like in *bubonic plague?* Like in *the black death?*"

"It's not conclusive," I said.

"I want one of those flea collars," Connie said. "Do they really work?"

"Fuckin' A they work," Lula said. "They sell them at Petco. They wouldn't sell them at Petco if they didn't work."

"Do you have any extra?" Connie asked her.

"I've only got this one 'cause I had to make sure it would fit, but I could make a Petco run and pick up a couple," Lula said. "What would you like on yours? Do you want the diamond look or do you want some color in it?"

"I think color," Connie said. "Something flattering to my skin tone. Maybe red."

"I don't want to bust anyone's bubble here," I said, "but the fleas could be hopping onto your feet and biting you in the ankle, and I don't think a flea collar on your neck is going to be much help."

"Ankle bracelet!" Lula said. "Everybody likes a ankle bracelet. I could hang a charm from it. A little heart or your initial."

"I'd like my initial," Connie said.

"This is big," Lula said. "I could be the next Martha Stewart. Martha's gonna be real angry that she didn't think of this. Although I have to say she makes a damn good laundry basket. And I got a stellar cake decorating book by her."

"I thought you didn't have an oven," I said.

"Well, yeah," Lula said, "but I got the book. Everybody should have that book. Just in case the occasion arises to make a cake and you got an oven."

"I have some new FTAs," Connie said. "They came in first thing this morning. Nothing big. Nuisance roundups if you haven't anything better to do."

As it happened I had nothing better to do, so I stuffed them into my bag along with Jesus Sanchez, the lawnmower bandit.

"I don't mind riding along with you while you pick up these losers," Lula said, "so long as we can make a Petco stop. And then I got to go to the craft store to get some charms and more jewels."

We took my car and did the Petco run first. After Petco we made a fast stop at the craft store.

"I can't wait to put this all together," Lula said when she was back in the Porsche. "I don't know if you noticed but I got a knack for embellishment."

"I noticed."

"Who'd Connie give you? Anybody fun?"

"I read through them while you were in the craft store. We have a drunk and disorderly, a shoplifter, and a guy who stole a snake."

"Say what?"

"It was a four-foot python, and he stole it from a pet store that sold exotic reptiles and birds."

"Throw that one out the window. I bet he got a house full of snakes. I'm not going near him. I don't care if he never goes to jail and Vinnie goes broke because of him."

"How about the shoplifter?"

"Sure. Where's this person live?"

I pulled the file out of my bag and gave it to Lula.

"Richard Nesman," Lula said. "He lives downtown. Trevor Court. I know that area. It's a street of nice townhouses."

For the most part shoplifters are an easy catch. They aren't usually violent and they aren't usually armed. This is even true for the professionals, like Skookie Lewis, who takes whole stacks of T-shirts and transfers them out of the Gap and into the trunk of his 1990 Eldorado for resale. Lula has been known to shop out of Skookie's trunk.

I parked in front of Richard Nesman's townhouse and paged through his file. He was fifty-six years old, retired, married to Larry Staples.

"You see I don't get that," Lula said. "I got traditional values. I mean what's this world coming to?"

"You don't think gay men should marry?"

"Hell, I don't care if they marry. I'm talking about the name. You get married and you take your husband's name. Everybody knows that. Otherwise it's too confusing. It's chaos, you see what I'm saying?"

"Yes, but what if they're both husbands?"

"Say what?"

"Gee, look at the time," I said. "We should get moving if we want to get all this done before lunch."

I went to the door to the townhouse and knocked, and a pleasant-looking silver-haired man answered.

"Richard Nesman?" I asked.

"Yes."

"I represent Vincent Plum Bail Bonds. You've missed your court date, and I'd like to help you reschedule."

"I'm sure that's a mistake," Richard said. "I have it on my calendar in big red letters. It's next Friday."

"The court thought it was last Friday," I said.

"That's very upsetting. They should at least notify you if they change your date."

Lula was standing behind me. "So what did you shoplift?" she asked him.

"Shoes."

"Like boxes of Air Jordans or something?"

"Good heavens, no. These were Salvatore Ferragamo Sardegna Crocodile Driving Loafers."

"Get out!" Lula said. "Those are excellent shoes. Those shoes retail at $2,400."

"How do you know that?" I asked Lula.

"Sometimes I moonlight selling shoes. I help Skookie with the night shift. You gotta know what you're selling." She turned to Richard. "I could get you those same shoes for twenty-four dollars. You just gotta be careful if you wear them in the rain 'cause the color might run."

"Is this your first arrest?" I asked him.

"Sadly, no. I'm afraid I have a compulsion to steal shoes. I like to think of it as a hobby, but not everyone sees it that way."

"Everybody needs a hobby," Lula said to him. "I like to bedazzle. You should switch your hobby to something more constructive like decoupage or bedazzlin'."

We left Richard with the docket lieutenant, picked up our body receipt, and returned to the office.

"I made some phone calls," Connie said, "and I found Jesus Sanchez. He's living with his sister on Maple Street. So far as I can see he doesn't have a job, so you might find him at home."

Lula and I drove to Maple Street and started reading off numbers. It's a long street on the north end of town and by the time we counted down to the Sanchez house we were just two blocks from Kiltman.

226

An older woman answered the door.

"He's not here," she said. "He's walking the dog. They like to go to the school so Frank can make poopie on the grass."

"Frank's the dog?" Lula asked.

"Yes. Big dog. Big black dog. Very nice."

We thanked the woman, went back to the car, and drove toward the campus. We cruised along the loop road and spotted Jesus and Frank sitting in the middle of the field, watching some students play Frisbee.

"Guess nobody told any of these people about the fleas," Lula said.

"There haven't been any reports of fleas or plague," I said. "I think Pooka is hiding somewhere, and I'm sure he'll be found before he has a chance to do any damage."

"You don't know that for sure. Pooka could be out at night sprinkling his bloodthirsty fleas all over the place. Just because he lost his fireworks don't mean he's given up on spreading the black death. I personally think they should be warning people."

"I'm sure if they thought there was a real threat they would be taking precautions."

"Not that it affects me," Lula said. "I got my flea collar on, and if I gotta walk across the grass to arrest that idiot out there I'm putting my ankle bracelets on, too."

I parked on the side of the road, and Lula pulled a flea collar out of its box and strapped it around her ankle.

"It don't make the same fashion statement as when you put a charm on it, but it still looks okay. This here is the minimalist version," Lula said.

Heaven help me, I couldn't figure out if Lula was genius smart or flat-out stupid for wearing the flea collars. At a very basic level they made sense.

"Okay," I said. "Give me a couple of the ankle-size collars."

I mean, what did I have to lose besides some dignity? Better safe than sorry, I told myself.

Lula and I got collared up, and we tramped across the lawn to Jesus.

"Are you Jesus Sanchez?" I asked him.

"Yes," he said. "And this is my dog, Frank." He shaded his eyes with his hand and looked up at Lula. "For a minute there I thought you were wearing a flea collar around your neck."

"This here's the latest in fashion accessories," Lula said. "I'm starting a business in bedazzling them."

"Are they expensive? My sister might like one. Do you need your lawn cut? I have a lawnmower."

"Neither of us has a lawn," Lula said. "And anyway we came to give you a ride."

I introduced myself and fed him the line about rescheduling his court date.

"I guess that would be okay," he said.

He stood, and when I tried to cuff him, he yelled *"Run!"* to Frank, and the two of them took off.

Lula and I ran after him, across the lawn. Lula lost steam and quit before she got to the loop road on the other side of the green space. I stuck with Jesus and

Frank, but I was tiring and they weren't. I chased them for a block and gave up. They were too fast, and the bond was too small. If I was determined to catch him I could stake out the sister's house, but at this point I couldn't care less about catching him.

I was bent at the waist, sucking air, and I saw a rusted-out, dented white van roll past. It turned at the corner and disappeared. I was pretty sure I saw Pooka behind the wheel. I walked to the corner and looked up and down the street. No van. I retraced my steps and I was halfway across the street on my way back to Lula when the van burst out of a driveway behind me. I jumped away, but the right front quarter panel clipped me, and I was punted about fifteen feet. I was caught totally off guard, feeling more shock than pain. I rolled onto my back, and I saw Pooka looking down at me.

"Look what fell onto the road," he said, holding my stun gun.

He pressed the prongs against my arm, and twenty-eight million volts sizzled through my brain.

A stun gun doesn't necessarily knock you out. It scrambles your neurons so you have no muscle control and there's a lot of confusion. When the confusion cleared I was in the back of Pooka's van, cuffed with what I assumed were *my* cuffs. I'd put the cuffs and the stun gun in my back pockets when I set out for Jesus Sanchez.

It was hard to tell what sort of damage had been done when I got hit. I had some stinging pain in my left knee and my jeans were soaked in blood. I wiggled my toes and moved my legs and nothing seemed broken.

No bones sticking out anywhere. My elbow was killing me but it was behind my back, and I couldn't see it. No headache. No double vision. I didn't land on my head. One bright spot in my day.

It was a panel van. No seats in the back. Just me rolling around every time he made a turn. Plus some cartons of firecrackers, a box of blasting powder, and a couple empty aquariums. At least they looked empty. I suppose there could have been a few carsick fleas hunkered down in the bottom of the cages. I had to wonder what he did with the fleas that used to be in the aquariums. Not a good thought. Also hard to have good thoughts about my immediate future.

The van stopped and I heard a garage door roll open. The van eased into the garage and the door rolled back down. I was trying not to panic. I was taking deep breaths, telling myself to stay calm and alert. I had to wait for my opportunity. It would come. And people would be looking for me. Ranger and Morelli. I trusted them to find me. They were smart. They had resources.

Pooka left the driver's seat, came around, and opened the back door.

"Fate," he said. "Amazing, isn't it? I'm driving down the street, and there you are. I was going to come get you, but you came to me."

He grabbed my ponytail and pulled me out the door. I fell off the bed of the van onto the garage floor, and he dragged me up by my armpits. My knee hurt, my arm was on fire, my elbow hurt, and I was breathing hard, trying to control the pain and not cry. I didn't want to cry. I didn't want to show fear or weakness. He pushed me in front of him, opened a side door, and pushed me into a grungy kitchen. Chipped red Formica countertops. Filthy linoleum floor. Decrepit stove and refrigerator. Stained avocado green porcelain sink filled with trash. Aquariums filled with fleas as far as the eye could see. The stench was sickening.

"Why does it smell so bad in here?" I asked.

"It's the smell of black death," Pooka said. "I've soaked the mice in contaminated blood and the fleas are feeding on them. Soon they'll be ready to release. I've got thousands of fleas in the bedroom that are infected. I released some of them earlier today. I was returning from the release when I came across you."

"It's not black death anymore," I said to him. "The plague can be cured with antibiotics."

"My plague is super bad," Pooka said. "I'm breeding super fleas, and I've mutated the plague bacilli. No one will survive. No one. My fleas will march across the Kiltman campus and lay waste to everything in their path."

"Like a little army."

"Exactly!"

"Why did you kidnap me?"

"You're a terrible person. You ruined my moment of beauty and surprise. Everyone's moment. I'm going to infect you and you will slowly the a horrible death. But before you the you're going to redeem yourself by feeding my fleas."

I looked around. The shades were drawn on all the windows.

"Where are we?"

"We're at the gates of everlasting."

He moved toward me with the stun gun. There was a flash of blinding light, and I crumpled to the floor. I felt him drag me across the kitchen into another room. I heard clanking and grunting. A door clicked closed and there was quiet. I struggled with the fog in my head, struggled to push through it. The room swam into focus. Small room. No furniture except for a mattress on the floor. My eyes adjusted to the darkness. There was a form on the mattress. It wasn't moving. I took a moment to breathe. To get myself together. I had feeling back in my arms and legs. I managed to sit. He'd changed the cuffs so my hands were in front of me now. A thick chain tethered me to the wall. I could move around a little but a padlock attached to my cuffs was also attached to the chain. The chain was bolted into the wall.

The form on the mattress moved, and I realized it was a person.

"Becker?" I asked.

"Unh," he said.

I moved closer and saw that his arms were full of needle punctures. Some in his upper arm and some over veins.

"Drugs," he said. "Make me tired."

His hands were cuffed in front like mine. He was also chained to the wall. His eyes were completely dilated. I wasn't sure if it was from the dark or the drugs.

"Crazy," Becker said, slurring the word. "Evil crazy."

I could hear Pooka moving around the house, mumbling to himself. Drawers opened and closed.

There was the smell of gas and then something burning.

"What's that smell?" I whispered.

"Bunsen burner," Becker whispered back. "Never works right. Probably because he's got it hooked up to bottled propane. Not sure what he does with it. Defrosts the mice for the fleas, I think. He left the door open yesterday and I could watch him boiling stuff and measuring it out. And he injects himself with something. I always thought he was creepy, but it's so much worse. He's completely insane." A tear slid down his cheek. "I think I'm dying."

"No way," I said, but honestly he didn't look good.

"He needed a blood donor for the fleas," Becker said. "He drugged me and chained me up in the garage and made me call my parents. And then there were always more drugs and I was so tired."

Pooka opened the door and came at me with the stun gun. "This makes everything so much easier," he said. "Say good night."

CHAPTER
TWENTY-FOUR

I awoke slowly with a throbbing headache. It took a full minute to orient myself. Kidnapped. Chained. Stunned. I looked at my arm. Two puncture wounds. One in the vein in the crook of my left arm. One in my upper arm.

"He took blood," Becker said. "And he drugged you. And he said he infected you. He said I should tell you so you'd know. I'm sorry."

"Where is he now? The house is quiet."

"He left. I heard him moving around out there and then I heard the garage door open and close. And I think I heard the van leave."

"How long ago?"

"I don't know. I'm confused."

I pushed myself up and fought back nausea that was as much from fear and horror as from the drug. I stood on shaky legs and managed to get to the wall. The bolt that the chain was attached to had been screwed into the wall and epoxy glue had been poured over it. I rapped on the wall. Sheetrock. I grabbed the chain with both hands and yanked. Little pieces chipped away around the bolt. I yanked again, putting my weight into it, and the bolt broke loose.

I stood there holding the loose chain in my hand and I burst into tears. Loud hysterical sobs.

"S-s-sorry," I said to Becker. "This is an emotional moment."

I wiped my nose on my arm and went to Becker's chain. I gave a tug, but the bolt held firm. I put one foot on the wall, leaned forward, and pushed off with every ounce of strength I could muster. The bolt broke free, and I fell over backward onto Becker. We both let out a *woof* of air on contact, and neither of us moved for a beat. I wrestled myself off him, and tried to get him up onto his feet but he was dead weight.

"Go," he said. "Leave me here."

"No way," I said to Becker. "You're coming with me if I have to drag you."

I grabbed him by the back of his shirt and dragged him out of the room and into the kitchen. Difficult to do because my hands were still cuffed. I stopped long enough to look around. The place had been cleaned out. No more aquariums. No Bunsen burner. Pooka had moved on and left us behind to die. Fortunately for us he's a lousy carpenter.

It was too difficult to drag Becker by his shirt so I got him by an ankle and tugged.

"Keep your head up," I said to him. "I don't want to go to all this effort only to give you a concussion."

I managed to get him out the kitchen door and into what might pass for a yard. It was mostly hard-packed dirt and scrub grass and garbage. The driveway leading up to the house was dirt, and we were surrounded by woods. I had no idea where we were. I tried getting

Becker up again, and he was able to stumble to the tree line. I walked him far enough into the woods so he would be hidden, and I left him there.

"I don't think Pooka is coming back," I said, "but stay hidden just in case. I'm going for help."

I limped down the driveway, got to a paved two-lane road, and still saw nothing but woods. No houses. No cars. No 7-Eleven. I had a dilemma now. If I heard a car coming, and I went out into the road to wave it down, I ran the risk of it being Pooka. No guarantee that he'd still be in the white van. Also no guarantee that anyone other than Pooka would stop. I looked like something from a horror movie. My one arm was covered in caked-on blood. My jeans were torn and blood soaked. My hands were shackled and the thick chain was still padlocked onto the cuffs. A small chunk of wallboard was attached to the end of the chain.

I was at the edge of the driveway, trying to decide to walk left or right and a black SUV came into view from my left. I stepped slightly into the road so the driver would be sure to notice me. I was fighting the drug and the blood loss, working to stay focused. The SUV slowed and stopped just short of where I was standing. Black Porsche Cayenne. Tank behind the wheel. Ranger out of the car and running toward me. I would have done more sobbing, but I didn't have the energy.

Ranger wrapped his arms around me and held me close against him. "It's okay," he said. "I've got you."

"How did you find me?"

He reached into the front pocket of my jeans and removed the key to the Macan. "GPS key tag," he said. "You had your car key with you."

"Becker is at the other end of the driveway. He's not in good shape. He's been drugged and had blood taken from him. And probably he's been infected with plague."

Ranger looked down at my arm with the needle marks.

"Me, too," I said.

"Babe," he said, so soft it was barely a whisper.

He took a universal handcuff key out of a pocket on his cargo pants and opened my cuffs. He looked at the chunk of wallboard still attached to the chain and raised an eyebrow.

"Pooka might be a brilliant biologist, but he doesn't know a lot about construction," I said. "If he'd drilled the bolt into a stud I couldn't have gotten free."

"I'm sure it still took some muscle to get this out of the wall," Ranger said.

"I was motivated."

Ranger tossed the cuffs and the chain into the back of the SUV, and Tank drove us up the driveway to the ramshackle house.

I led Tank and Ranger to Becker, and we got him out of the woods and unshackled. Tank folded the backseat down and stretched Becker out in the Cayenne cargo area. Ranger and Tank did a fast walk-through of the house. We left Tank on the property to wait for Rangeman backup to arrive, and to keep everything secure until the police took over. Ranger, Becker, and I left in the SUV.

"Did you call Morelli or did you call dispatch?" I asked Ranger.

"I called dispatch. Morelli is unavailable."

"Did Lula call you?"

"Lula called *everybody*. Fortunately I was on the list because no one else would have thought of the key fob. You could also have been tracked through your phone, but you left it behind in your messenger bag."

"I ran out of pockets."

The woods disappeared after a half mile, and we were in a lower income neighborhood of small bungalow-type houses.

"Where are we?" I asked Ranger.

"South Trenton. This street runs into Broad. Blatzo lives one street further south. We'll be at St. Francis in less than ten minutes."

I looked back at Becker. His eyes were closed. His breathing seemed regular.

"How's he doing?" Ranger asked.

Becker kept his eyes closed, but he gave me a thumbs-up.

"He's doing great," I said.

"Tank will have called ahead. The hospital should have someone waiting for us at the ER entrance. How are you doing?"

"I'm okay. Slight headache. Probably a drug hangover. Or it might be my life. He stunned me and injected me with something that had me out for a couple hours. Becker said that while I was out Pooka took blood from me and infected me with plague."

I took a moment to breathe and pull myself together. It was hard to stay calm about the plague.

"What about the blood caked on you?"

"I was chasing an FTA and Pooka came out of nowhere and bounced me off the front of his van. He got to me while I was still dazed, and he used my cuffs and stun gun to immobilize me. When I came around I was in the back of the van." I looked at my arm. "I think it's all surface scrapes and bruises. At least it's stopped bleeding."

Ranger swung into the drive to the ER entrance and stopped in front of the doors. Two uniformed Rangeman guys were waiting for us, plus a nurse with a gurney, and a bunch of men in badly fitting suits.

"Who are the suits?" I asked Ranger.

"CDC, FBI, EPA, Homeland Security, Trenton PD."

"I'm surprised Morelli isn't representing the Trenton PD. He's the principal on the murders."

"Word is he's getting a colonoscopy."

So maybe I didn't have such a bad day after all. At least I didn't get something stuck up my butt.

We off-loaded Becker onto the gurney, and I walked beside him, holding his hand into the building.

"You're going to be okay," I told him. "Even if you are infected with the plague, it's treatable now."

"My parents . . ."

"You need to call them. I know they'll want to see you and make sure you're okay."

"I haven't got a phone. Pooka threw my phone away. He was worried about being traced through it."

Ranger was standing behind me. "I'll have Hal get a phone to him."

"And Gobbles," Becker said. "I need to talk to Gobbles. I should have listened to him. He said to stay away from Pooka."

Becker was wheeled off into an examining area and two of the suits walked with him.

Susan Gower was the charge nurse on duty in the ER. I went to high school with Susan and smoked my first and last joint with her.

She came over to me and grimaced. "You look like you got hit by a truck."

"It was a van," I said.

"Do you want to have someone look at whatever it is that's wrong with you?"

"No," I said.

"Yes," Ranger said.

"Boy," she said, looking Ranger up and down, "if I wasn't happily married —"

"I've just got a few scrapes," I told her.

"Yeah, I can see that," she said. "Come on back. I'll put you in a room and get someone to clean you up. If you need stitches you want to get them sooner rather than later. Later doesn't work."

The room was actually a small space separated from a lot of other small spaces by privacy curtains that didn't give you much privacy. I filled out a lot of paperwork, waited a half hour for something to happen,

240

and finally a nurse came in with a pair of scissors and cut my jeans off above my knee.

"Omigod," she said, "what's that on your ankle? It looks like a flea collar."

I'd forgotten I had them on. They were hidden under my jeans. Ranger was sitting in a plastic chair on one side of the bed. He didn't move, but his attention went to the flea collar and it drew a smile.

"You can cut it off," I said to the nurse. "I have one on the other ankle, too."

It was after six by the time I had all the pieces of gravel picked out of my cuts and abrasions and everything was cleaned and bandaged. I'd needed ten stitches under my elbow. I got a tetanus shot. I had blood drawn. I was started on antibiotics. And I was told to return if I developed symptoms.

Three guys in suits were slouched in more of the plastic chairs in the waiting room. They all stood when I finally limped out of the examining area, and they all handed me their cards. Chris Frye, CDC. Chuck Bell, FBI. And Les Kulick, Homeland Security.

"I'd appreciate it if you would come downtown to give a statement," Bell said.

"I've been run over by a van, stun gunned at least twice, injected with some sort of narcotic, and there's a good chance I've got bubonic plague," I said. "Today isn't a good day."

"Yeah, I can see that," Bell said. "It'll wait."

Ranger moved me out of the building, and one of his men drove up with the 911 Turbo. Ranger took over behind the wheel, and we left the hospital grounds.

"I'm going to take you home with me," Ranger said. "I don't feel comfortable leaving you alone in your apartment tonight."

This was perfect. I didn't want to be alone in my apartment. I was exhausted and scared and my elbow was killing me. There would be food in Ranger's kitchen and silky soft sheets on his bed. The air would be cool and clean and not smell like dead mice soaked in plague blood. And I'd have Ranger next to me making me feel warm and safe.

"I'd love to stay at Rangeman tonight," I said, "but I might not be up to a lot of romantic stuff."

"That works for me," Ranger said. "Nothing personal, but I'd rather not exchange any bodily fluids until I do more research on the plague."

He called ahead to tell his executive housekeeper, Ella, we were on our way home, and I would be spending the night, and that I needed some necessities. Ella and her husband manage the building and food service. Ella knows me, and she knows my sizes. She outfits everyone at Rangeman, and that's included me on the occasion when I've worked in uniform for Ranger. Everything from shoes to underwear to jeans and a shirt would be waiting for me in the morning if not sooner.

By the time we got to Ranger's apartment on the top floor of the Rangeman building, my knee was scabbing over, and I was barely able to bend my leg. I was anxious to get out of my bloodstained clothes, so I borrowed a T-shirt and sweatpants from Ranger and hobbled into his bathroom.

I stood in his Zen shower until I felt clean again and the sick odor of Pooka and his house was out of my head. I washed my hair with Ranger's Bulgari shampoo, and carefully patted my scraped and bruised body dry with one of his fluffy bath towels. I found some big Band-Aids in his bathroom linen closet and patched myself up. I pulled the sweatpants on and cinched in the drawstring. I dropped the nice comfy too-big T-shirt over my head. I was a new woman.

I padded barefoot to the kitchen and wrangled myself onto a counter stool.

"Wine," I said. "I need a glass of wine. White and cold."

Ranger took a bottle out of his under-the-counter wine cooler and uncorked it. He poured out two glasses, gave me one, and kept one for himself.

He clinked my glass. "To Wonder Woman," he said. "I'm impressed. You didn't need me to rescue you today."

"No, but I'm glad you did."

We drank some wine, and Ella knocked on the front door and came into the kitchen with a tray of food. Bread basket, New Zealand lamb racks, herbed vegetables cooked al dente, and fresh fruit for dessert. She set the tray on the counter and handed a shopping bag to me.

"Let me know if this isn't right," she said to me.

I looked in the bag. Black Pilates pants, black T-shirt, black undies, black Converse sneakers.

"Perfect," I said. "This is really nice. Thank you."

She smiled and a little color came into her cheeks. "You're the only lady who visits," she said. "I enjoy doing the shopping."

Ella left, and we ate in silence until I pushed my plate away.

"That was delicious," I said.

Ranger stood and moved the plates from the counter to the sink. "Ella brought fruit, but I have ice cream in the freezer."

"Yes! Ice cream."

I used Ranger's phone to call Gobbles.

"I found Becker," I said.

"I know," Gobbles said. "I just got off the phone with him. He sounded weak. He said he was worried he had the plague."

"I'm sure they're doing tests and giving him antibiotics. He's not showing any symptoms, so if he has been infected it's in an early stage."

I was saying this as much to reassure myself as to reassure Gobbles. I needed to believe I'd be okay. I didn't want to think for a single moment that I might die from the plague.

"Now that Becker is safe we need to get you back into the system," I told Gobbles. "If I take you in tomorrow morning there's a good chance that we can get you rebonded and released by the afternoon."

"Sure," Gobbles said. "Should I go to the courthouse or do you want to pick me up someplace?"

"I'll pick you up at Julie's house tomorrow at ten o'clock."

244

I disconnected with Gobbles and Ranger gave me a bowl of ice cream.

"You should call Morelli," Ranger said. "I'm sure he's thinking he picked a bad day for a colonoscopy."

"Is there ever a good day?"

Ranger selected a slice of apple from his fruit plate. "Not on my calendar."

I called Morelli's home number and cell number and he didn't pick up either. I left a message on both telling him I was fine and with Ranger for the night.

"Babe," Ranger said, "that's not a reassuring message. If I were Morelli and I just had a colonoscopy, I'm not sure I'd want to know you were spending the night with me."

"We aren't exactly a couple anymore."

"Had me fooled," Ranger said.

I finished my ice cream and could barely keep my eyes open.

"I'm done," I said to Ranger. "I'm going to bed."

"I have paperwork to do, and I need to check on some things downstairs," Ranger said. "I'll be in later."

CHAPTER
TWENTY-FIVE

I felt Ranger leave the bed, and I looked at the time. Five-thirty. Ranger's day started early. I heard the shower running, and I drifted back to sleep.

It was a little after eight o'clock when I finally made my way to the kitchen in my new clothes. The Pilates pants had been a good choice. The material was soft and stretchy over my scabbed-up knee. A decanter of coffee, a bagel and cheese plate, and fresh fruit had been set out on the counter for me. The coffee was still hot. I helped myself to breakfast and found a note from Ranger telling me the Macan was in the garage and the key was in the glove compartment, and that Lula had my messenger bag. The note had been propped up against the little plastic container of antibiotics I'd gotten at the hospital.

I took one of the pills and washed it down with coffee. I brushed my teeth and tried to ignore the large scrape on my face. It's just skin, I told myself. It'll grow back. And besides, it takes the attention away from the pimple that's almost all gone.

I took the elevator to the control room and went to Ranger's office.

"I'm heading out," I told him. "I had breakfast, and I took my pill. I'm set for the day."

"Seeing you in those pants makes me wish I'd taken a chance on exchanging fluids," Ranger said. "Be careful. Pooka is still out there."

"If he's already infected me, what more could he do?"

"He could shoot you," Ranger said.

With that in mind, I descended to the garage, found the Macan, and drove to the office.

Connie looked up when I walked in. "Boy, I'm glad to see you. We were really worried when Lula couldn't find you. She walked all around the neighborhood and finally found someone who said a lady had been hit by a white van and taken away. I guess they thought the guy in the van was taking you to get medical help."

"He tagged me with my stun gun, handcuffed me, and loaded me into the back of his van. How could that possibly be interpreted as medical help?"

"It was a little kid," Connie said. "The kid said the nice man gave you bracelets."

The front door banged open, and Lula burst in.

"I got it. Heaven help me, I got the plague. I woke up and I was all itchy, and when I got to the bathroom I saw them!"

"Saw what?" Connie asked.

"The boo-boos. I got them. They're all over me. I'm gonna die. I got plague boo-boos."

"Have you been to a doctor?" Connie asked.

"No. I came straight here. I'm afraid to go to a doctor. He's gonna tell me my fingers and toes are gonna fall off and then I'm gonna die. I read about it, and it's not good to the from the plague. I'm gonna need a closed casket. I'm gonna look terrible. And I'll tell you another thing. I want my money back on those dumb flea collars. They don't work."

"Where are the buboes?" I asked her.

"All around my neck and ankles."

Connie got up and took a close look. "You've got a rash from the flea collars."

"I never thought of that," Lula said. "I guess I should take them off. I even wore them in the shower, and come to think of it they got all sticky."

Connie gave Lula scissors, and Lula cut the flea collars off and threw them away.

"This here's a big relief," Lula said. "I thought I was a goner." She looked over at me. "Holy cow, what's with you!"

My hand went to my face. "You mean the scrapes and stitches?"

"I mean the Pilates pants and the little black T-shirt. That's a total new look for you. It's damn sexy. I might try that look on myself."

"It's comfortable," I said. "The material doesn't pull on my scabs."

"We got an abbreviated version of yesterday from Tank," Connie said. "And Susan Gower called and said you came in for some stitches, but you were okay."

"I got some skin taken off when Pooka hit me with the van. I was lucky I wasn't hurt worse."

248

"Tank told us you were with Becker."

"Pooka had been keeping Becker in the garage behind his house by Kiltman. I think he moved him when he moved the fleas."

"Why'd he want Becker?" Lula asked.

"Pooka needed a blood source for his fleas," I said. "He had Becker drugged, and he was taking blood from him."

Lula's eyes rolled back into her head, and she crashed to the floor.

"Either she just had a massive heart attack or else she fainted," Connie said. "Get her feet elevated."

I propped Lula's feet up on a couch cushion, and Connie draped a wet towel over her forehead.

Lula opened her eyes, but she looked like she was still out.

"No blood," she said. "You can't have my blood."

"No one's taking your blood," Connie said. "You fainted."

"Did I pee my pants?" Lula asked. "I heard sometimes you pee your pants when you faint."

We got Lula up on her feet and moved her to the couch.

"I didn't actually faint," Lula said. "I just had a moment. You better not tell anybody I fainted. It would ruin my reputation for being sensitive but tough."

"I've got your messenger bag from Lula," Connie said to me. "I put it in the bottom file drawer."

I retrieved my bag and pulled my phone out. Twelve missed calls from my mother and four from Morelli. I didn't want to talk to either of them. I didn't know what to say.

"I'm picking Gobbles up so he can check back in with the court," I said to Connie. "Hopefully we can get him rebonded right away, so he doesn't have to spend a night in jail."

"Vinnie's there now. I'll tell him to wait for you."

"I'll go with you," Lula said. "And on the way back we can stop at a drugstore, and I can get some cortisone cream for my neck. It's already feeling better now that the flea collar is off. Except I feel underdressed without my bedazzles."

Gobbles was waiting on the sidewalk in front of Julie's house when I pulled up. He got in the backseat, and he looked nervous.

"I hope this goes okay," he said. "I don't want to be in jail. It's scary when they close the door, and you're behind bars like a caged animal."

"Vinnie is there now," I said. "We'll do everything we can to get you released."

Ten minutes later I parked in the public lot, took Gobbles directly into the courthouse, and turned him over to Vinnie.

"He's going to be okay," Lula said. "I got one of those feelings again."

I dropped Lula off at the drugstore, and Morelli called while I was waiting for her.

"I got a hospital report on you," he said. "Are you okay?"

"I'm good. I just have to wait to see if I get sick."

"I'm not going to ask about last night," he said. "I don't want to know."

"Nothing happened. I had a horrible day, and it didn't seem like a good idea to leave me alone in my apartment."

"I guess I can identify. I had a colonoscopy."

"I heard. How are you doing?"

"I'm doing great," Morelli said. "I'm sorry I wasn't there to help you yesterday."

"As it turned out, it was lucky you weren't available. When you didn't answer Lula's call, she went to Ranger, and he was able to track me down. I was driving a Rangeman car, and I had the GPS key fob in my pocket."

"I heard you got run over by a truck."

"I was looking for an FTA and Pooka came out of nowhere and clipped me with his right front quarter panel. Have they found him yet?"

"Not that I know. Everybody and their brother is looking for him."

"He must have had a contingency plan. As soon as the fireworks were discovered and confiscated, he was out of his apartment by the college and into another house. And he moved again after he captured me. He drugged me, drew blood for his fleas, supposedly infected me with plague, and he packed up and took off."

" 'Supposedly infected'?"

"If I let myself believe it I get hysterical."

"Any idea where he went?"

"No," I said. "No idea at all."

"I'm kind of sidelined today, but I'll be back at work tomorrow, and I might be able to find out more. Are you staying at Rangeman again tonight?"

"No. I'm going back to my own apartment. Rex gets lonely when I'm away."

Lula returned to the car and I said goodbye to Morelli.

"Who were you talking to?" Lula asked. "Did you get any more information about Pooka?"

"I was talking to Morelli. He's off today, so he doesn't have much information."

"We heard he was having a colonoscopy. I don't know why anyone would want one of those. First off you get a camera stuck up your butt. A camera! It might as well be a rhinoceros."

"It's a small camera," I said.

"Don't matter. It's a camera. Not only do you gotta get it stuck way up there, but it takes pictures. I mean do you want people looking at pictures of the inside of your butt? Isn't it bad enough everyone's looking at the *outside?*"

"It's not like it gets put on YouTube."

"You don't know that for sure. And that's not even the worst part. I read about it. If they see something sticking out on the inside of your butt they knock it off with the camera. If you got one of them polyp things the camera knocks it off. And then what happens to it? Do they stick a vacuum up your butt and suck the polyp up? I mean how much stuff can you stick up there, right?"

252

I turned the radio on. Loud. If the radio didn't drown Lula out I was going to crash the car into a telephone pole.

"What are we going to do now?" Lula yelled at me. "Do you want to go after the lawnmower man?"

"I'm taking the afternoon off. I need some downtime."

"I get that. Me, too. I've been traumatized by my flea experience. And that's my word of the day, by the way. *Traumatic*. I thought it was an appropriate word of the day. I bet I get to use it a lot today."

I dropped Lula at the office and I turned into the Burg. No doubt my mother had already gotten a bazillion phone calls about me getting checked out at the hospital. I needed to show her I was okay, and it was all not a big deal. It would take some acting on my part, because it felt like a big deal to me. I was thinking that maybe I should give the pastry chef thing one more try.

I parked in the driveway and tried not to limp on my way to the front door. My knee hurt, and my elbow didn't feel all that good, either. My mother was in the kitchen ironing. Never a good sign. My mother ironed when she was upset. She'd iron the same shirt for hours if she had nothing else to iron. My grandmother was at the kitchen table on her laptop.

"Tweeting?" I asked her.

"Nope," she said. "I'm checking out bubonic plague. We heard you got it. And I have to tell you I'm not finding much good about it."

"I don't have the plague. I feel fine."

My mother looked up from her ironing and made the sign of the cross. "Good heavens, just look at you!"

"I don't think she looks that bad," Grandma said. "I was expecting a lot worse. I saw this movie once where a guy got dragged down the road behind a pickup truck and Stephanie don't look nearly that bad. And her pimple looks a lot better than it used to."

"I thought I'd stop around for lunch," I said. "I'm starved."

"Hear that, Ellen?" Grandma said. "You can stop ironing now."

"In fact I have a terrific idea," I said. "Let's go out for lunch."

"I don't know," my mother said. "I'm not dressed."

"We don't have to go someplace fancy," I said. "We could go to the diner on Route 33 or we could go to Cluck-in-a-Bucket."

"I vote for Cluck-in-a-Bucket," Grandma said. "And I don't want drive-thru food, either. They screw you at the drive-thru. I'm going to get a double Clucky Burger with bacon and cheese and special sauce. And I'm going to get cheese fries."

"You'll be up all night with heartburn," my mother said.

"I never get heartburn," Grandma said. "You're the one that gets heartburn. I'm going to get my purse."

My mother unplugged the iron, Grandma returned with her purse, and I loaded everyone into Ranger's Porsche Macan and drove to Cluck-in-a-Bucket. Cluck-in-a-Bucket is on the edge of the Burg. It's fast food at its best. Cheap, greasy, and salty. The building is

254

yellow and red inside and out, and on weekends some kid desperate for money dresses up in the Clucky suit and struts around the parking lot. Everyone in Trenton, either sooner or later or all the time, eats at Cluck-in-a-Bucket.

CHAPTER
TWENTY-SIX

I parked in the Cluck-in-a-Bucket lot, and we all went in and ordered our food. I got two pieces of chicken and a biscuit, my mother wimped out with a salad and grilled chicken strips, and Grandma went full on with the double Clucky Burger.

"This is nice," my mother said. "We should do this more often."

"I agree," Grandma said. "It's good to do things like a family. Going out to eat is so civilized, too. You get to sit and relax and enjoy your food and you don't have to do the dishes after."

We were in a booth by a window, and I looked out and saw Lula pull into the lot and park. She got out of the Firebird and waved at me on her way to the door.

"I was driving by on my way home and I saw your car here," Lula said. "It's a good idea to have lunch out like this. Do you mind if I join you? I don't want to horn in on a family outing."

"Of course you can join us," Grandma said. "Go get your food. We just got started."

Lula came back with a bucket of chicken parts and a bucket of biscuits.

"It's good to see Stephanie getting out after her *traumatic* day yesterday," Lula said. "Everything happened to Stephanie yesterday. First off, she wasn't watching where she was going, and she got hit by a van."

"I was watching," I said. "And it wasn't just any old van. It was Stanley Pooka's van. I saw him drive by and I went to look for him. He must have pulled into a driveway or, for all I know, he could have been in someone's backyard. Anyway I went to cross the street and he came roaring out and ran me down."

"Who's Stanley Pooka?" my mother asked.

"He's an idiot college professor at Kiltman," Lula said. "He was building fireworks in one of the fraternities there, so he could fill them with bubonic plague-infected fleas and shoot them off over the campus. Then the fleas would jump on people and give them bubonic plague and everyone would die." Lula buttered a biscuit. "Actually everyone might not die. Some people might just have their fingers and toes and dicks drop off."

"How would a man tinkle if his dick dropped off?" Grandma asked.

"It would be a problem," Lula said. "I guess he could tinkle like a lady."

My mother was speechless. She had her fork halfway to her mouth, and she was frozen.

"Wait a minute," my mother finally said. "This man, Stanley Pooka, intentionally hit you with his van?"

"He sort of clipped me with his right front quarter panel," I said. "It wasn't a direct hit."

"And that's how you got all these scrapes and cuts?" she asked.

"That wasn't even the worst of it," Lula said. "He kidnapped her and took her to a house where he kept his fleas. He had another guy there, too, and he was sucking the blood out of him to give to the fleas."

"He wasn't *sucking* the blood out," I said. "He was using a syringe."

This wasn't going well. I'd wanted to take my mom to lunch to get her calmed down. I'd wanted to give her the facts so she wasn't upset by exaggerated rumors.

"Let's talk about something else," I said. "I'd like to relax and enjoy my lunch."

"No," my mother said. "I want to hear about this. What happened to the man who was giving his blood to the fleas?"

"His name is Becker," Lula said. "He's a college student, and Pooka kidnapped him, too. And when Stephanie got there she rescued Becker and then Ranger rescued her."

My mother was holding her fork so tight her knuckles were white, and her eyes were scary looking. "What happened to Pooka?" she asked.

"He got away," Lula said. "Everybody's looking for him, and I don't know how anyone can miss his beat-up white van. I bet you anything he's riding around distributing his plague fleas, right under the nose of the FBI. He's like the invisible man."

"Do you really think the fleas got the plague?" Grandma asked.

258

"Sure they got the plague," Lula said. "And everyone they suck on is going to get the plague. Trenton's going to be known as the plague capital."

"No one knows if the fleas have actually been infected," I said. "So far no one has shown any symptoms of the plague. We're waiting for lab test results."

Waiting was an understatement. My stomach was sick with dread that the tests would be positive.

"We need to go proactive," Lula said. "We should be out there helping the police look for Pooka. I bet we could find him. You just gotta think like Pooka. And then I can use my extra perception to fine-tune it."

"His plan was to shut the college down," I said. "I can't see him moving away from that plan. It was an obsession."

"Yeah, but there's cops all over that campus now," Lula said. "They got people in uniform and people in street clothes. And I'm sure the kids and the faculty are all looking for him. No one wants to get bubonic fleas."

"So he's being sneaky," I said. "He's probably parking his van where it's hidden, and then he goes to the campus in disguise and distributes his fleas. He gets in and out fast."

"He might even be in a different car by now," Grandma said.

"I'm sure the police have thought of all those things," my mother said.

"Yeah, but they don't have my special skills of sensoring," Lula said. "I say we go on a manhunt!"

"I'm with you," Grandma said. "Let's go hunting."

"I have ironing to do," my mother said.

"The ironing is all done," Grandma said. "There was no ironing to begin with."

"I guess it wouldn't hurt to ride around the loop road," I said, "but I don't think we should get out of the car. We don't know where he's already dumped fleas."

"Exactly," Lula said. "When we spot him we call the police."

We finished eating and trooped out to my Macan. My mother sat in the front, next to me. Lula and Grandma took the backseat. I drove across town and turned onto the Kiltman loop road. I drove slowly so we could scan the campus. Nothing turned up on the loop road, so I wound my way up and down the smaller roads that led to dorms and classroom buildings and fraternities. I honestly didn't expect to find Pooka but it gave us all an activity, and I knew Grandma and Lula would have nagged me until I drove them around.

"Try some of the side roads," Lula said. "The ones with regular houses. If it was me, that's where I'd park on account of there's trees to hide you from helicopters looking for you. And those houses have garages that might be empty."

I drove off campus and into a neighborhood of faculty and student housing. I was cruising down a street that was completely shaded by old growth oak trees and I spotted a van on the next block. It wasn't white but it was the right shape and had an appropriate amount of rust and dents. Someone had clearly taken spray-paint to it, so that it was a mix of brown, green, and tan.

I parked just short of the corner. "Someone call the police," I said. "I think they should check this out."

"It's him," Lula said. "I know it's him. My Lula Sense is humming. I'm getting vibes all over. I'm going to take a look."

"Not a good idea," I said. "Wait for the police."

"It's okay," Lula said. "I got my gun."

"I'm going with you," Grandma said. "I got my gun, too. Don't look, Ellen. Pretend you didn't see that I got a gun."

"No!" I said. "Do *not* leave this car."

Too late. Lula and Grandma were already out of the car and creeping up on the van.

"Good heavens," my mother said. "What are they doing? Your grandmother is going to get herself killed."

"Stay here," I told my mother. "I'll go get her."

I got out from behind the wheel and ran to Grandma. I pulled up next to her, and the back door of the van flew open, and Pooka jumped out. His hair was dyed black and buzzed short but everything else was the same. Same stupid amulet. Same stupid pajama pants. Same insane glazed-eyed expression.

"You!" he said, glaring at me. "What are *you* doing here? You're supposed to be chained in the house. Not that it matters because you're going to die." His face was red and veins were bulging in his neck. "*Die!*" he screamed at me. "*Die!*"

He threw a glass jar that smashed about ten feet in front of us. Close enough that I could see fleas flying out everywhere. Thousands of them.

"Dirtbag," Grandma said, and she fired off four rounds at Pooka.

All four rounds missed Pooka, but Lula had her gun out, too, and she was blasting away at him.

Bang, bang, bang!

"Did I hit anything?" she asked. "I forgot to bring my glasses when I changed my purse."

Pooka jumped into the van and took off.

I hobbled to my Macan and got behind the wheel. Grandma and Lula scrambled into the backseat.

"Don't let him out of your sights," Lula said. "You can catch him."

I didn't want to catch him. I wanted to keep my eyes on him, so the police could catch him.

"Call police dispatch," I said to Lula. "Tell them what's happening. And then call Rangeman. They can track us by my key fob."

Pooka drove out of the neighborhood and turned onto Olden Avenue. There were six cars between us, but I was sticking with him. He turned off Olden onto a newly paved road that led into a light industrial park. I knew the area, and I knew the industrial park was bordered at one end by woods. If he got to the woods it would take a lot of manpower to find him. There were no cars between us now. I floored the Macan and caught up to him. I was looking in my rearview mirror, hoping to see police lights, but it was just the two of us on the road.

262

I could feel everyone leaning forward, eyes glued to the van. No one was saying anything. We were all in the moment. Focused. We were all aware that this wasn't trivial. This man in front of us could be spreading bubonic plague, and he had to be stopped. It was up to us.

The van sped ahead, and I followed. I was two car lengths behind. Lula was on the phone with the police. The road in front of me was straight, and we were almost at the entrance to the industrial park. Taillights flashed in front of me as the van came to a screeching stop. I stomped on my brakes, but I smashed into the van. Everyone in the Porsche was thrown against their seatbelts, and the air bags went off. I fought my way free of the airbag and saw that the front of the Macan looked like an accordion. Totally smushed, steam coming out of the radiator.

"What the hell was that about?" Lula yelled.

"He stopped short," I said, breathing heavy after getting hit with the air bag. "I think he did it to wreck our car so we couldn't follow, and he did a good job of it."

"He can't get away with that," Lula said.

She leaned out the back window and fired off six shots into the back of the van. I heard *Pop! Pop! Pop!* and *Zing! Wannng! Bang!*

"Omigod," I said. "He was carrying fireworks back there. And blasting powder!"

I tried to back up, but the Porsche was stuck to the van, hung up on its back bumper.

"Everyone out of the car!" I said. "Now!"

We all scrambled out of the car and saw that Pooka was also out of the van and running for the industrial park entrance.

"Get him!" Grandma yelled. "Get the bastard."

I thought this wasn't a bad idea because we didn't want to be near the van if it still held blasting powder.

We took off after Pooka, and we were about fifty feet down the road in front of the van when it exploded. *VAROOOM!* A black mushroom cloud erupted from a huge fireball that consumed both vehicles. Tires and chunks of fiberglass sailed through the air.

Everyone stopped, including Pooka. We all paused, utterly gobsmacked for a moment, and then Pooka took off down the road at a run.

I hobbled after him, Lula was huffing and puffing beside me, and Grandma was a couple paces behind us. My mother was off like a shot.

I was shouting *"Stop! Stop!"* and Grandma was shouting *"Go, Ellen, GO!"* My God, I thought, what's my mother thinking? What will she do if she catches him?

"She's gaining on him," Lula said. "Who would have thought she could run like that?"

"She ran track in high school," Grandma said. "She was pretty good."

My mother was about three feet from Pooka. She threw herself forward, grabbed hold of his shirt, and they both went down to the ground. They rolled around a little and by the time I reached them, my mother was on top, punching Pooka in the face.

264

"She's beating the crap out of him," Lula said. "Way to go, Mrs P."

I pulled my mom off Pooka before she killed him, and Lula sat on him to keep him from running again. Police cars were turning onto the road, lights flashing. They paused behind the burning vehicles and slowly went off-road around them.

Trenton PD was first on the scene. Ranger and Tank were close behind in a Rangeman SUV. Two fire trucks and an ambulance followed. Pooka was bleeding from the nose, his right eye was swelling, his shirt was torn, and his power amulet had gotten ripped off his neck. My mom was a little dusty, and she had a skinned knee, but otherwise she looked okay.

Lula got off Pooka and turned him over to one of the cops.

"What happened to him?" the cop asked.

"He tripped while he was running," Lula said. "It was these baggy pajamas he's wearing. They're good for letting your boys breathe while you're watching television, but you don't want to run in them, what with your nuts knocking around in there."

"This is Stanley Pooka," I told the cop. "The FBI and Homeland Security people will want to talk to him. And I think he'll tie into Morelli's three homicides."

"That was righteous," Lula said to my mom. "You kicked his ass."

"I did!" my mother said. "I was pissed off. He hit Stephanie with his car, and she, got all scraped up. He could have killed her."

The cop walked Pooka past my mom on the way to the patrol car, my mom kicked Pooka in the back of the leg, and Pooka went down to one knee.

"Hey, lady," the cop said, hoisting Pooka up, "you can't do that. He's in custody."

"Sorry," my mom said. "Restless leg syndrome."

Ranger ambled over. "I'm guessing that the smoking, molten black lump in the road back there used to be a Porsche Macan."

"It wasn't my fault," I said.

Ranger cut his eyes to Pooka getting loaded into the cop car. "Looks like you made a good apprehension."

"It was my mom. She took Stanley Pooka down like a junkyard dog on a piece of rancid meat."

Ranger grinned at my mom. "Never underestimate maternal rage."

Another Trenton PD car drove up. Eddie Gazarra was behind the wheel, and Morelli was riding shotgun. Morelli got out and walked over to us.

"I thought you were taking the day off," I said to him.

"I heard this called in and I didn't want to get cut out of the bust. Was anyone in that mess back there when it caught fire?"

"Not that I know. Someone could have been in the back of the van, but I didn't see anyone."

"From what I'm piecing together, you saw Pooka and followed him here. Somehow both vehicles caught fire. It looks like he got out and ran and you chased him down and beat the crap out of him."

"He fell when he was running," I said.

266

"It was on account of his nuts were loose," Lula said.

Morelli looked at Lula and then he looked at me. "There's no way in hell I'm putting that in my report."

"You have a thing about nuts lately," I said to Lula.

"I like nuts," Grandma said. "I like cashews."

I looked down at Morelli's feet. "You're wearing two different shoes."

"I was in a hurry to get out of the house."

"Pooka threw a jar at us. It was filled with fleas and it smashed on the 300 block of Oak Street," I said to Morelli. "You might want to have it exterminated or something."

"I'll call it in," Morelli said.

"Now that we blew something up and captured the dirtbag I could use some ice cream," Grandma said. "We didn't get to have dessert."

"Good thinking, Granny," Lula said.

We all turned and looked back at the twisted, charred disaster that used to be a van and a car.

"Uh-oh," Lula said.

Ranger handed me the keys to his SUV. "I'll have someone come get me. Tank and I need to stay and make funeral arrangements for the Macan anyway."

I drove Ranger's SUV back to Cluck-in-a-Bucket. We all got ice cream sundaes and took them to the booth by the window.

"Good thing I took my purse when I got out of the Macan," Grandma said. "We couldn't have bought these sundaes otherwise."

My mother, Lula, and I had exited fast and left our purses behind. Tomorrow I'd be going to get a replacement driver's license and a new messenger bag.

"I understand why you do your job," my mother said to me. "There's a sense of accomplishment when you take down someone bad. It's like being a police officer or being in the Army or being a mother. You have a responsibility to protect and keep order, and you do whatever it takes to get that done." My mother spooned into her ice cream. "I got a real rush out of it, too. I liked hitting him."

"Yeah, we could see that," Lula said. "You were a wild woman."

"I have my moments," my mother said.

I dropped my mother and grandmother off, and I was heading for home when I spotted Lula's red Firebird in my rearview mirror. I pulled over and stopped and she ran up to me.

"I saw him," Lula said. "I saw the lawnmower guy. He's cutting grass on Lime Street. I was going across town to get a new driver's license and there he was plain as day. You should go get him. It'll be easy."

Lime Street wasn't far away. Five minutes tops. Jesus Sanchez wasn't a big ticket bond, but his capture would pay for a new messenger bag. I turned around and took Liberty Street to Lime with Lula following me.

I parked when I saw Sanchez, and Lula parked behind me. I searched through Ranger's stash of weapons and helped myself to cuffs and a stun gun. Lula got out of the Firebird and crossed the street with me. Sanchez didn't see us or hear us. He was busy cutting grass. I walked directly behind, reached around, and clamped a bracelet on him. He looked at the bracelet and jumped away from the mower.

"He's gonna run," Lula said.

I saw the panic in his eyes and knew she was right. He turned from me and Lula tackled him. I got the second cuff on him, and as soon as Lula rolled off I pulled him up to his feet.

"Who owns the lawnmower?" I asked him.

"The lady in the house."

We left the lawnmower by the lady's front door and loaded Sanchez into the backseat of the SUV.

"I can handle it from here," I said to Lula.

"That's good," Lula said. "I can continue on then and get my driver's license and a new purse."

"The DMV is on the other side of town."

"I don't go to the DMV. Nobody does that anymore. I go to Otis Brown in the projects. I don't have to stand in line and it only costs five bucks."

"You get a fake driver's license?"

"Yeah, but it's a good fake. You can't tell the difference. And I can put a flattering picture on it. And on top of that he always has a good selection of handbags in the trunk of his car. It's one-stop shopping."

An hour later I was back at the office trading in my body receipt for Sanchez, getting a check for the capture in return.

"How did it go with Gobbles?" I asked Connie. "Was Vinnie able to get him released?"

"It wasn't necessary. Charges were dropped against Gobbles. Insufficient evidence. Mintner's injury wasn't consistent with getting hit with a baseball bat. Plus, it's not like Mintner is here to testify against Gobbles."

"According to Julie, Mintner was obsessed with closing Zeta and created the incident to use as one more strike against the fraternity."

"I was curious so I did some digging," Connie said. "Mintner had a record of dirty tricks against Zeta. In his own way he was just as crazy as Pooka. I guess some of his craziness was justified. I found a newspaper article from a couple years ago about a scandal at Kiltman. Faculty wives had been going to parties at Zeta, and two of the wives ended up getting pregnant by a Zeta. Both Zetas involved were underage so there was a big legal mess. The women were able to avoid jail time but both of them were eventually divorced. One of those women was Ginger Mintner, Mintner's wife."

"Bummer."

"Yeah. I heard you took down Pooka today."

"Actually it was my mother who took him down."

Connie grinned. "Lula told me. She called a couple minutes ago. She was calling from her home phone because Otis couldn't get her new phone activated until tomorrow."

"Do you know Otis?"

"Everyone knows Otis."

CHAPTER
TWENTY-SEVEN

I was stiff and sore when I woke up. It was eight o'clock Wednesday morning. The sun was shining. Crazy Pooka was locked away. All I had to worry about was bubonic plague. I didn't have a fever. No swollen lymph nodes. All positive signs. I looked out my bedroom window into the parking lot. More happy news. Ranger's SUV was still there. I was on a roll. The dumpster forklift hadn't carted it away. It didn't look like it was full of geese. It had all its tires.

I limped into the kitchen and put a frozen waffle into the toaster. I started coffee brewing and I made a mental list of things I needed to do. Get a driver's license, buy a phone and a messenger bag, replace stun gun, handcuffs, and pepper spray, find more Pilates pants, check on Becker.

I called Connie and told her I was taking a day off to organize myself. She said she'd gotten a call from Susan Gower saying that Becker was looking good and going home with his parents today. That was a relief. I was happy for him and even happier for myself. If his fingers and toes hadn't fallen off yet maybe I'd get to keep mine awhile longer.

I spent three hours in line, waiting to get a replacement driver's license. I would have cut out after two hours and gone to Otis but I didn't know where to find him and I didn't have a phone so I couldn't call anybody. By five o'clock I'd gotten the license, bought a new messenger bag and four pairs of black Pilates pants, and had my new phone activated. I'd swapped out my jeans for one of the Pilates pants, and my knee was feeling much better.

It was close to six when I finally drove into my apartment building's parking lot and saw Morelli's green SUV with Morelli lounging against it. He looked over and smiled when he saw me.

"I've been calling you all day," he said.

"I didn't have a phone. It burned up in the Porsche. I just got a new one, and I had to get a new number."

He pulled me close and kissed me. Lots of tongue and some groping in broad daylight in my parking lot. His hand moved over the stretchy Pilates pants, feeling up my ass.

"No underwear," he said.

"Jeez Louise! We're in the parking lot. I can see Mr Zajak hanging out of his window."

"Don't care. What's with the no underwear?"

"They're Pilates pants. You're not supposed to wear underwear with them."

"I like it."

"I can tell. Holy cow, Morelli."

"Let's get married. Do you want to get married?"

"Omigod," I said. "You're going to die. You only have two days left."

272

"Do I look like a man who's going to die?"

"No. You look really healthy. Maybe too healthy."

"So what do you think? Do you want to go upstairs and consummate our impending marriage, or would you rather go to dinner?"

"What kind of dinner? The diner? Pino's? The Grille?"

"Anywhere you want."

"I'll take the Grille. I should change into something nicer."

"Cupcake, those pants aren't coming off until I take them off."

"Okay, then, I guess I'm ready to go. Your car or mine?"

"We'll take my car. Your cars have a twenty-four-hour expiration date."

The Grille is a relatively new restaurant on Hamilton. Previously too expensive for me, but apparently Morelli wasn't watching his budget tonight. It's cozy inside with dark brick walls and polished wood floors. White linen tablecloths and candles on the tables. Morelli ordered a steak and baked potato and a glass of red wine. I did the same.

"It looks like your stomach is feeling better," I said.

"Yeah, I'll tell you about that later. I have lots of other news for you. Stanley Pooka hasn't stopped talking since we took him into custody. Some of it is nonsensical babbling, but a lot of it is good. As you know, his research was rejected for funding, and he was passed over for tenure. I think he didn't have a good grip on things before that and that helped push him over the edge. He talked a lot about his obligation to cleanse the ground Kiltman was built on. He said the amulet told him to contaminate it with plague."

"Did the amulet tell him to shoot Getz?"

"No. He thought of that all by himself. Getz went into the cellar to check on some extermination work and he went nuts over the fireworks. At that point in time Pooka didn't have any other place to work. His apartment was filled with flea cages. So he shot Getz."

"Makes sense to me," I said. "What about Linken?"

"Basically the same thing. Linken was at Zeta the day of the Getz viewing to discuss a fraternity scholarship program. Someone mentioned the flea problem in the cellar, and Linken wanted to check on it. Pooka was licensed because he was forced to walk across campus and let Linken into the cellar. Linken took one look at the fireworks and threatened to bring endangerment charges against Pooka."

"So Pooka shot him."

"Yeah."

"Wouldn't it have been easier just to move the fireworks operation?"

"Pooka started moving some of it. From what we can tell from the incinerated van, he had some firecrackers and blasting powder in the back. The thing is, I think Pooka was finding it easy to shoot people. *Bang!* Problem solved. He wasn't all that logical by the time he shot Linken. His mental health wasn't helped by the fact that he was injecting himself with a concoction that hasn't been completely analyzed. It contained blood

274

and a hallucinogen and God knows what else. It was supposed to make him immune to the plague."

"Oh boy."

"He said he shot Mintner because Mintner was nosy. He caught Mintner trying to break into the cellar, chased him outside, and shot him."

"No one noticed?"

Morelli gave a small head shake. "We've interviewed a lot of people and no one noticed. It was like that sort of thing happens all the time at Zeta parties. There was a band playing and everyone was drinking and no one noticed."

"The band was pretty good," I said.

"Yeah, I know the band, but the drummer is no Brian Dunne."

"That's what Lula said!"

"Anyway, we found Pooka's gun, and it all checks out."

"That's great. You've solved your murders."

"The best part is coming up. Pooka had been obsessed with Unit 731 for a long time. Especially the use of plague as a military weapon. If you search back through his papers and computer history, it's all there. He also had a history with a third-rate biotech lab in Maryland. He'd worked there off and on while he was in grad school, and he knew they kept some unsavory and illegal things in their freezers. Things like a couple rats that were supposedly infected with plague."

"Why would they keep those rats in their freezer?"

"I guess initially the rats were sent to them for testing, but through sloppy housekeeping the rats were mis-placed or something. Anyway, time passed, the rats were never tested, and they stayed in the freezer. Pooka knew about them, and one day he went in and dropped them into his raincoat pocket and walked off with them. If he'd looked into it a little more he would have found that the reason the rats weren't tested was because no plague had been found in the area where they were trapped."

"There's no plague?"

"Looks that way. At least not in Trenton."

I choked back the rush of emotion. I had my hands clasped tight in my lap, and my teeth sunk into my lower lip. I didn't want to burst into tears in the restaurant. I was half-afraid that once I got started crying I wouldn't be able to stop. It didn't matter that I was crying because I was so happy. I wasn't an attractive crier. My nose would run and my face would get blotchy and people would stare.

"Jeez," I said, pausing a beat to get my voice under control. "I'm really relieved."

Morelli nodded. His eyes were dark and serious, and his voice was soft. "Me, too," he said. "I'm sorry I didn't tell you sooner. I thought the hospital called you."

We clinked our glasses in a silent toast, and we both chugged our wine. The waiter rushed over and refilled our glasses.

"Okay, so there's no plague," I said. "How could Pooka make a mistake like that? Didn't he do any of his own testing?"

"By the time Pooka went to get the rats he was not in a good place."

"He seemed odd, but he didn't seem insane when I first met him."

"People said that about Jeffrey Dahmer. Remember him? He was the guy who worked in a candy factory and kept decapitated heads in his freezer."

"Like Blatzo."

"Blatzo didn't work in a candy factory," Morelli said. "Even if there had been plague in the rats or in the fleas Pooka was breeding, the blood cocktail he was feeding the fleas probably would have killed the bacilli. He thought he was breeding super fleas but the lab tests suggest he was doing the opposite. None of the fleas that were found and tested were infected."

"I'm not going to suffer the agony of the plague."

I said it with a smile. I couldn't stop smiling.

"So what about you?" I asked Morelli.

"Xanthan gum."

"Excuse me?"

"I can't digest xanthan gum. I thought I had cancer. My doctor thought I had Crohn's disease. My Sicilian grandmother said I was cursed. I've been through a month of testing. I've been on a restrictive diet. And it turns out the restrictive diet was the worst thing. I was eating tons of gluten-free bread, and it all contains xanthan gum. So I was getting worse instead of better."

"How did the colonoscopy turn out?"

"The colonoscopy was the best thing that happened to me. Not only am I perfect inside, but I haven't had any xanthan gum in three days and I feel great."

"How did you find out about the xanthan gum?"

"I was working with an allergist along with a bunch of other doctors and the allergy panel just came back."

"You're allergic to xanthan gum."

Morelli cut into his steak. "Actually it's a sensitivity, but it acts like an allergy. I can eat meat and drink wine. I just have to read labels and stay away from food additives. And it's not stress. It's not my job, and it's not you." Morelli sat back and grinned at me. "I'm cured. So do you want to get married?"

"I don't know. Do you have a ring?"

"No. Do I *need* a ring?"

"My mom will expect to see a ring."

"Since I don't have a ring maybe we can get engaged to get engaged."

"What would that involve?"

"It would involve getting you out of those Pilates pants. Unless you'd like to stay for dessert."

"I guess I could skip dessert."

Morelli looked around and caught the waiter's eye. "Check!"